D0253350

The Divine Ryans

WAYNE
JOHNSTON

The Divine Ryans

VINTAGE CANADA
A Division of Random House of Canada Limited

Vintage Canada Edition, September 1998

Copyright © 1990 by 1310945 Ontario Inc.

All rights reserved under International and Pan-American Copyright
Conventions. Published in Canada by Vintage Canada, a division of
Random House of Canada Limited. Originally published in hard-
cover in Canada by McClelland & Stewart Inc., in 1990. Distributed
by Random House of Canada Limited, Toronto.

Vintage Canada and colophon are registered trademarks of Random
House of Canada Limited.

Canadian Cataloguing in Publication Data

Johnston, Wayne, 1958–
The divine Ryans

ISBN 0-676-97184-9

I. Title.

PS8569.O3918D58 1998   C813'.54   C98-932234-3
PR9199.3.J63D58   1998

Cover design by Jonathan Howells

Visit Random House of Canada Limited's Web site:
www.randomhouse.ca

Printed and bound in the United States of America

10 9 8 7 6 5

For my sisters,
Cindy and Stephanie

1

OUR HOUSE must be sold to help keep *The Daily Chronicle* afloat. What better place for Aunt Phil to make this announcement than in the graveyard, among relatives who, by the way she looked at their headstones, might all have died to keep the *Chronicle* afloat? To hear her talk, giving up the house was the least that we could do.

"Their only regret," said Uncle Reginald, "is that they have but one house to give for the *Chronicle*."

We had moved in with Aunt Phil three months ago, supposedly so that the house that we were renting from her, at what Uncle Reginald called "the family rate," could be repaired. The repairs were taking place, all right, but we would not be moving back, not ever. Aunt Phil said that we could stay with her as long as we liked. All of her children had moved out, so there was plenty of room, she said. The rest of us said nothing, and no wonder. When someone tells you that your house is being sold to help preserve the life work of your great-grandfather, at whose grave you just happen to be kneeling, there isn't much you can say. Except maybe "We who are about to lose our home salute you," which was what Uncle Reginald had said ten years ago upon being told that *his* house must be sold.

Lots of things had been sold to keep the *Chronicle* afloat. We had once owned a marbleworks and a pair of flower shops, but these had been sold. Other houses had been sold. Uncle Reginald swore that Reg Ryan Sr. had bought up all the houses on Fleming

Street just so that in re-selling them he could pick and choose his neighbours. Fleming Street was what Reg Ryan had made it, Uncle Reginald said, a little empire, all of which had been left to Aunt Phil, and most of which was now gone. Uncle Reginald had taken his disinheritance better than anyone expected. After the reading of Reg Ryan's will, he had turned to Father Seymour and said: "Well, at least he let me keep his name."

All that was left of the empire, except for Aunt Phil's house, was its four corners: the *Chronicle* and the funeral home, which we owned, and the orphanage and the convent, which we might as well have owned, given how long someone named Ryan had been running them. *The Daily Chronicle*, Reg Ryan's (as the funeral home was called), St. Martin's orphanage, and St. Mary's convent. The only money-maker in the lot was the funeral home, prompting Uncle Reginald to remark that, from now on, the family motto should be, "We make our living from the dead."

Because there were so many priests and nuns in the family, we were known throughout the city as the Divine Ryans. We had always been a church family, and had married into other church families, so that it sometimes seemed that all the priests and nuns in the world were related to us. Our last family re-union, Uncle Reginald said, was known to the rest of the world as Vatican II.

Aunt Phil's news was that much harder to take because our old house was next door to hers. I could see it from my bedroom window. In fact, because the curtains were down, I could see right into the rooms, all of which were empty. One night, I stood there for a long time, looking at our house, wondering who would move into it. Almost directly across from my new bedroom window was my old one, where I had often stood, looking out at Aunt Phil's backyard, hoping to catch a glimpse of Aunt Phil escorting Uncle Reginald to the hearse.

I looked away from the window. On the wall of my room was a picture of me which Uncle Reginald had had blown up. The original had appeared in *The Daily Chronicle* about a year ago when I had been chosen minor hockey player of the week, an honour I would not have had bestowed upon me if, on the one hand, my father had not been editor-in-chief of the *Chronicle*, and on the other, if he had ever seen me play. In the picture, I was dressed in full goalie gear, face mask included. I looked like some sort of insect, magnified ten thousand times, preening for the microscope. At my skates, on the ice just in front of me, lay my nemesis, the puck. The word "puck," my father had once told me, originally meant "demon." For a time it had even been used interchangeably with "hobgoblin." I made a mental note of thanks to that anonymous inventor of hockey who had had the good sense to opt for "puck."

I looked back to the window again, and was surprised to see that in the house across the way the kitchen light was on. The kitchen looked—there is no other way of putting it—as if some-one was about to enter it. For a few minutes, there was no sign of anyone, but then came a faint flickering of shadow as if, in a room just off the kitchen, someone was moving about. The flickering stopped for a few minutes, then began again, more distinct this time, as if whoever was making it was coming closer. Finally, from out of the darkness of the house, he appeared, look-ing as if he had just come home from work. My father stood at the kitchen sink and looked out the window, at me, it seemed, though he gave no sign that he had seen me. I closed my eyes, then opened them to find that a man unmistakably my father was still staring at me, a look of forlorn perplexity about him as if he could not understand why we had left him behind when we moved. Then he took from his coat pocket what looked like a hockey puck, which he began to toss from hand to hand, his head going back and forth as he followed the flight of the puck through the air. Then he held the puck to his ear, shaking it now and then, as you might do with a watch to see if it was ticking. Backing away from the window, I turned and ran downstairs.

"Mom," I shouted, "Mom, Dad is in our house. In the kitchen. He's there, I saw him."

"Jesus, Mary, and Joseph," Aunt Phil said, blessing herself as she got up from her chair and ran to the dining room, from which the view of our old house was much the same as from my bedroom. My mother and Father Seymour also stood up, Father Seymour doing his best to look calmly amused, stretching out one arm towards my mother as if to assure her that they could both sit down.

"I saw him," I said. "I did." Aunt Phil came back and gave me that look she always gave me when I misbehaved. She looked at me as if I had been put on earth for some dark purpose, my ignorance of which was my only blessing.

"Lies," Aunt Phil said, as if, despite the haste with which she had run to the dining-room window, she had known all along that I was lying. "Nothing but lies."

"I saw him," I said. "The light was on and he was looking out the window. He had a puck—"

"There's not even a light on over there," Aunt Phil said.

I ran to the dining room and looked out the window, only to find that what she said was true. The house was dark, which meant that no one would believe that I even thought that I had seen him, let alone that I really had. I ran back to my mother. "Mom, I saw him," I said. "I did." My mother put her arms around me, holding my head tightly to her stomach, as much to silence me as to comfort me, it seemed, for when I struggled to get free, she held me tighter. "I saw him," I said.

"Shutup, Draper Doyle," said my sister Mary, who believed it was all an obvious, if tasteless bid for attention, a commodity which she seemed to think no nine-year-old could ever get enough of. I looked at Uncle Reginald, who winked at me, whether to assure me that he believed me or that he thought the joke was in poor taste was hard to say.

"I won't have this sort of behaviour in my house," Aunt Phil said, looking down at me. Here I was, holding my mother, whose waist felt as if Aunt Phil could close one hand around it, and here was Aunt Phil, standing over me, looking as if I could not have enclosed her with both arms. I imagined trying to do so, my face lost in Aunt Phil's bosom as I struggled to get my arms around her, Aunt Phil standing to full height to make it more difficult for me, impassively resisting me as she might have some temptation of the flesh, standing erect, her expression one of righteous satisfaction, as if her great girth was the very measure of her virtue.

"I don't want Draper Doyle going to any more wakes," my mother said. "No more wakes, Aunt Phil."

At first, Aunt Phil looked shocked. Then she pressed her lips tightly together and said, as if to no one in particular, "You'd think it was my fault the child was seeing things."

"I'm sure that's not what Linda meant," Father Seymour said, in a way that made it impossible to tell whose side he was on.

"No," my mother said. "No, of course not. I just—"

"If this is the thanks I get," Aunt Phil said, "for taking in my brother's whole family—"

I was about to point out that she wouldn't have had to take us in if she hadn't taken our house from us in the first place, but Sister Louise intervened. "Linda was just upset," she said, looking at me as if she believed I had lost whatever children had in the way of sense. Sister Louise had been confined to a wheelchair since some early childhood accident. Her black boots, on the footrest of her chair, might have been skates from which the blades had been removed. "We're all upset," she said. At this, there was much nodding of heads, as well as a kind of general retreat, everyone shifting about to indicate that the unpleasantness had passed.

"Sit down here beside me, Draper Doyle," my mother said. I sat on the sofa between her and Mary. Soon, Aunt Phil, Father Seymour, and Sister Louise were presiding, like some Vatican-appointed committee, over the question of my visitation. Aunt Phil said it was preposterous to even think that a grown man would appear to his nine-year-old son instead of to his wife or to his sister. My mother, declining this invitation to join with her against me, said nothing.

Uncle Reginald told Aunt Phil that knowing more about visitations than other people didn't make her any more likely to have one. "Of course not," Aunt Phil said, "but neither should fanciful nine-year-olds be taken seriously." Aunt Phil, who considered herself something of an expert, had often held forth on visitations. She was constantly expressing the fear that her own husband would visit her, appear at the foot of her bed in the middle of the night to deliver some awful message. Her dead husband's name was never spoken, by her or by anyone else. People said He or Him if mention of him was unavoidable. You understood who they meant, because you could hear the capital H, their tone faintly mocking that of Aunt Phil, who said He or Him with such fearful reverence that people unsure of who she meant were known to bless themselves. Aunt Phil claimed that, although she had yet to be visited, her husband had often been present in the house, invisibly present, performing little acts of mischief. All household mysteries were attributed to Him. If she could not remember the name of someone she had known for years, it was His doing. Once, when she broke a teacup, she said, "That was Him did that," as if her dead husband had wrenched it from her hands.

Now she looked pointedly at me. She informed me that people came back from the dead to deliver "messages" or "warnings" to the living, not just to look at them or, "of all things to throw pucks up in the air. "When They come back," she said, "They come back. There's no maybe They did or maybe They didn't." I was about to say that there was no maybe in my mind when, this time, Uncle Reginald spoke up. He said that if the dead came back to warn the living against having too much fun, it was extremely unlikely that Aunt Phil would ever be the subject of a lecture from beyond the grave. At this, Aunt Phil looked to Father Seymour and Sister Louise to come to her defence.

"Draper Doyle has often heard you talk about visitations, Phil," Father Seymour said. "That's probably where he got the idea." Again, there was much nodding of heads, as if to say that Father Seymour had put his finger on it, exactly on it. In the process, he placated Aunt Phil, restoring her to her place as foremost authority on visitations. Aunt Phil even seemed faintly pleased with me, smiling at me as if to say that I could not be completely lacking in sense if I had been so strongly affected by something she had said. Father Seymour's words had put me in a new light, it seemed. I was neither liar nor usurper of authority, just a nine-year-old boy on whom, without even knowing it, she had had a profound influence.

"I'm sure Draper Doyle wasn't telling lies," Aunt Phil said. "It's just that he misses his father, which is understandable." This, then, was the finding of the committee, that, while no visitation had taken place, my claiming that one had was understandable.

Later that night, when everyone was gone to bed, I stood at the window again, looking out at the house across the way. It appeared to be as dark and as empty as when I had last looked. I wondered if my father might still be there, in one of the rooms, hiding from us. It seemed like the kind of thing he would do.

I thought of my mother and Aunt Phil, standing side by side at his grave earlier that week. "His death was your punishment, my dear," Aunt Phil had said, though not by way of accusing my mother of anything in particular. She was just as apt to say that her own husband's death had been *her* punishment. It was one of the inscrutable ironies of Aunt Phil's God that he spared the person with whom he was displeased and took some blameless relative instead. To Aunt Phil, my mother was a kind of novice widow, her husband but five months dead. She wanted her to do what she had done, embrace widowhood as her vocation, her calling. For this was what Aunt Phil believed, that God had made them widows for a purpose, that a kind of dark sacrament had been extended to them.

"I don't want you taking him to any more wakes," my mother had said. In fact, I had not been to a wake since my father's, about which, I was happy to find, I remembered nothing. Even the days leading up to my father's death had been blanked out. My "missing week" Uncle Reginald called it. My father, he said, was gone but not forgotten. My missing week, on the other hand, was forgotten, but not gone.

I wondered how many more times we would gather in the graveyard to hear bad news. There were two things I hated about my father's headstone. First, there was my name. Whatever chance I had had of convincing people that my name was Draper, not Draper Doyle, was gone now that "Draper Doyle" was on the headstone, for how could you change something that was literally carved in stone? Doyle was my second name, and it was because my father had, for some reason, been fond of calling me by both names that my mother had deemed it appropriate that the headstone read "sadly missed by Draper Doyle." I complained, of course, pointing out that they didn't call Mary "Mary Louise" and wondering why my father had been fond of "Draper Doyle." It wasn't as if there were so many Drapers in the family that he had to use second names to tell us apart.

The other thing I hated about the headstone was that my father's day of birth and day of death were the same. He had died on his birthday, the worst of all possible days on which to die, it seemed to me, though that was not how the others chose to see it. Uncle Reginald told me that in his eulogy, Father Seymour had said that you could think of my father's life as a circle, a journey from birth to rebirth. "God gave Donald's life a perfect shape," Father Seymour said.

I climbed into bed and looked again at the picture of me on the wall. In the darkness, I could barely read the caption which Uncle Reginald had written on the bottom border of the picture. "Draper Doyle: Goalie," it said. It looked more impressive than it had when the light was on, more imposing. There I was, weirdly oversized in my equipment, looking out at the world through my face mask. The puck at my feet might have been a symbol of the fate of all pucks that came my way. That, at any rate, was how I chose to think of it as I fell asleep.

2

I T BECAME a kind of routine for me, standing at the window, watching the empty house across the way grow dark. Twice in the next couple of weeks, my father appeared in the kitchen exactly as before. First I discovered that the light was on, then saw a faint flickering of shadow, as if, in one of the rooms just off the kitchen, someone was moving about. Then he appeared, though in fact it was less dramatic than that—he simply walked in, his jacket on his arm, his tie loosened, as if he had just come home from work. Each time, from out of his coat pocket, he produced a hockey puck, though he did not toss it from hand to hand or hold it to his ear as before, but held it tightly in the palm of one hand which he moved up and down, as if he was trying to guess the weight of the puck, or as if, about to throw it, he was wondering what sort of projectile it might make, assessing its possibilities.

Each time I saw him, I ran downstairs, shouting to the others, only to be embarrassed again, only to find that, from the dining-room window, no light was visible across the way. The second time, I convinced my mother that we should go over and take a look. With Aunt Phil, keys in hand, leading the way, with everyone doing their best to sound exasperated and not at all apprehensive, we walked over to the house, on the front steps of which Aunt Phil's resolve seemed to falter somewhat and, affecting complete contempt for the proceedings, she handed the keys over to my mother, who led us through the house, turning the lights on one at a time, showing me, with a flourish of her hand, that each room was empty. At the end, the whole house was lit up, even the basement, and there was no sign of anyone having been there but the carpenters. Not even the kitchen showed any sign of my father having been there. I searched among the rubble on the countertop, thinking that perhaps he had left the puck behind, but found nothing. "I hope you're satisfied, Draper Doyle," Mary said as, one by one, my mother turned off the lights and we went back home.

My mother suggested that what I needed was professional counselling of some kind, a psychiatrist perhaps. But Aunt Phil and Sister Louise agreed that, rather than have some stranger fill my head with "heaven knows what sort of ideas," Father Seymour would "look out" for me from now on.

Exactly what "looking out" for me would entail I discovered the next night, when Aunt Phil announced to everyone that I was now a member of Father Seymour's Number. I looked to my mother to save me from this fate, but she said nothing, only looked at Father Seymour and gave him the same wincing smile she gave him whenever he made one of his supposedly flattering remarks. Father Seymour had the reputation of being, as Aunt Phil proudly put it, a "charmer with the ladies." That is, he was known to indulge in a kind of playful ribaldry with the older ones, especially those who were widowed or unmarried, a kind of mock flirtation that many of them found hilarious and even encouraged. "My dear," he'd say to some woman, whose husband was twenty-five years dead, "if I wasn't wearing this collar, I'd marry you myself." With our mother, it never quite came off. "My dear," he'd say, when she appeared in her best dress, "I wouldn't mind chasing you around the block." It never got the kind of laugh it did with the other women, perhaps because my mother was so young, so recently widowed, and perhaps because her wincing smile conjured up an all-too-vivid image of her running for her life from Father Seymour, a man about half her height whose white socks somehow made his feet look even smaller than they were.

My mother had yet to join what Uncle Reginald called Father Seymour's Other Number, that coterie of widowed and unmarried females from Fleming Street whom he escorted en masse to such parish functions as bingo games and fall fairs. Aunt Phil, who was herself a member, and Sister Louise wanted her to join, and seemed mystified by her reluctance. As for my mother, by the way she looked whenever the subject arose, she might have been an old maid and Father Seymour some absurdly inappropriate suitor whose attentions she was being pressured to repay by a family that was anxious to get rid of her. She tried to be polite, to seem flattered by the attentions of a man who, on top of being her brother-in-law and a priest, was, as Uncle Reginald somewhat too strongly put it, twice as old and half as tall as she was.

It was fast becoming one of those cherished family notions that some sort of special relationship existed between our mother and Father Seymour. He had taken to dancing with her at parties. Others who wished to dance with her made a great show of asking his permission first. Because of the difference in their height, they looked a little absurd while dancing together. Perhaps, Uncle Reginald said, if two holes were cut in the floor and a pair of soleless shoes put over them, our mother could stand in the holes, appear to be wearing the shoes, and finally be the right height for Father Seymour.

Despite Uncle Reginald, everyone was charmed by them. "There they are," their smiles seemed to say, "the brave young widow and the gallant priest." There was much talk about what great friends they were, "really" were, people said, by way of assuring one another that, while such relationships were often coy and affected, this one was not. That my mother did not go along with it except to the point of not offending Father Seymour hardly mattered, since people took whatever she did as confirmation of their view of things. Her embarrassed awkwardness with Father Seymour was taken to be just the kind of bashful modesty that was proper in the circumstances.

What went through my mother's mind when Aunt Phil announced my membership in Father Seymour's Number is hard to say. After smiling at Father Seymour, she looked a little panicked, as if she knew that unless she spoke up soon it would be too late, but, on the other hand, could think of no graceful way to decline, even on my behalf, something so highly esteemed among the family as membership in Father Seymour's Number. When she looked at me, I shook my head frantically, at which she cast down her eyes and, blinking rapidly, began fingering the neckline of her dress.

"Draper Doyle in Father Seymour's Number," Sister Louise said, as if to say, "Of course, why didn't I think of that?" Facing Father Seymour, she began to applaud, but stopped abruptly when no one but Aunt Phil joined in. Who better to counsel a young boy than a priest, said Sister Louise, especially when the priest was not only the boy's uncle but a man whose life work was counselling young boys.

Aunt Phil explained that from now on I would go to school at the orphanage, which wouldn't be that much of a change for me, since my present school was also run by Christian Brothers. I would, of course, continue to live at home.

"Isn't it reasonable to expect," Uncle Reginald said, "that boys at an orphanage be orphans?"

"Draper Doyle is half orphaned," Mary said, pointing out that this was appropriate since I would only be spending half my time at the orphanage.

"Very funny, Mary," I said.

I tried desperately to think of a way out. The last thing I wanted was to be a member of Father Seymour's Number, which was a group of one hundred orphans, trained by Father Seymour in the arts of dancing, singing, and, least appealing of all, it seemed to me, boxing. Someone had once said in *The Daily Chronicle* that Father Seymour's Number was, to the local church, what the musical ride is to the Mounties—"the showpiece of the order, the epitome of excellence." I was quite certain that I was, in no sense whatsoever, the epitome of excellence. My childhood to date should have been proof enough that I was definitely not the kind of boy that people would pay to see perform on stage, or anywhere else for that matter.

There were boys of all ages in Father Seymour's Number. Each year, as the oldest boys graduated from the orphanage, certain select newcomers were added to the Number, so that they were always, as Father Seymour put it, "one hundred strong." The Number was quite well-known throughout the city, usually taking first prize at both the music festivals and the boxing tournaments. There was often an item about them in *The Daily Chronicle*. "Father Seymour's Number To Perform At St. Martin's Hall." How often I had seen photographs of them, Father Seymour posing with his Number, the boys dressed as choirboys or dancers in one picture and as boxers in the other. It was only natural that singing and boxing go together, Uncle Reginald said, for after a certain number of low blows, anyone could be a choirboy. "Toughness of body, soundness of mind, purity of soul," was the motto of Father Seymour's Number. These were the qualities that he was trying to develop in his boys, his orphans whose lives would otherwise be shapeless, lacking in discipline and purpose. Father Seymour and his Singing Boxers, Uncle Reginald called them, describing them as a cross between the Vienna Boys' Choir and the Hitler Youth. It was the only choir in the world, Uncle

Reginald said, whose members had cauliflower ears and broken noses.

"I can't join Father Seymour's Number," I said, trying to achieve a kind of matter-of-fact finality of tone, as if it was literally impossible for me to join.

"I should like to know why not?" Aunt Phil said.

I told her I planned to try out for the hockey team, and would therefore have no time to be a member.

"On the contrary," she replied, "it's hockey that you'll have no time for."

"But I want to play hockey," I said.

"Well," Aunt Phil said, "you can't have everything," as if joining the Number had been my idea in the first place.

"I want to play hockey," I said again, this time standing up.

"Never mind about hockey, young man," she said, assuring me that there would be time enough for "leisure" in the next life. I should think of it this way, she said. Had I heard of the expression "earning one's rest?" Well, my reward in the afterlife would be an eternity of rest which, no matter how much work I did in this life, I could never fully earn. I could spend every second of my life working, she said, and heaven would still be more than I deserved. But why, I wondered, did I have to box and sing and tap-dance to earn my eternal rest? Why couldn't I do something else, like play hockey? I pointed out that I had no talent for singing, boxing, or tap-dancing. "Nonsense," Aunt Phil said, "of course you do," as if I had claimed to have no talent for breathing.

"You don't have any talent for hockey, either, Draper Doyle," Mary said. "It's not like you're giving up a great career."

"Draper Doyle in Father Seymour's Number," Sister Louise said, as if this would be the headline in tomorrow morning's *Daily Chronicle*.

"It takes a while to become a full-fledged member, of

course," said Father Seymour, who did not look as if the whole thing had been his idea.

"Oh, of course," Aunt Phil said, as if this was understood, yet looking a little disappointed. Sister Louise stared at him as if waiting for an explanation.

"But I think," Father Seymour said, glancing at Sister Louise, and then at my mother, "that we'll have him in the chorus by Christmas."

"Imagine," said Sister Louise. "In the chorus by Christmas."

She and Aunt Phil shook their heads, marvelling as much at me as at Father Seymour, as if I was already in the chorus, as if I was Father Seymour's latest miracle, already accomplished.

✦

"It's not like you're giving up a great career," Mary had said. Later that night, looking out the window, I had to admit that this was true. I loved, in fact lived and breathed, hockey, but I was not very good at it. I loved the Montreal Canadiens, the Habs, who possessed the kind of talent that defied all reason, who enjoyed the kind of spectacular, prolonged success that no one could explain. I was not normal in my fascination with the Habs, Mary said. "Even for a boy," I was not normal. I had played goal since the age of six, not because I preferred it, but because I couldn't skate well enough to keep up with other boys my age. On the wall of my bedroom, the one opposite the picture of me, arranged in chronological order, were pictures of all the goalies who had ever played for the Habs, a line of succession beginning with George Vezina and ending with Gump Worsley, the Gumper. Not only did the photograph show the changes in equipment worn by goalies, beginning with the spindle-thin, all-but-naked Vezina and ending with the well-padded Gump Worsley, but also, quite by accident, they seemed to demonstrate the ever-increasing tendency of goalies to stand erect, starting with the crouching Vezina and ending with the completely upright Gumper. The wall was like one of those charts that show the evolution of some species over eons of time. From cro-magnon goalie to goalie erectus in a mere one hundred years.

Whoever might come after Gump Worsley in that line of succession, I was fairly sure that it would not be me. Last year had been my first in organized hockey. The only time I had actually been in goal had been during the warmup to the first practice of the season. I subscribed to the little-known dodge ball school of goaltending, which was founded on the economy of pain principle, which stated that if it would hurt more to stop a shot than to let it in the net, you should let it in. In short, I played as if the point of playing goal was to keep the puck from hitting me. I became known as the Holy Goalie, as much because pucks seemed to go straight through me as because I was one of the Divine Ryans.

The coach had pointed out that Gump Worsley's lifetime goals against average was 2.65. The first digit of my goals against average was also 2, he said. Unfortunately, the decimal point did not come after it. It wasn't long before he devised a way to cut down on my goals against. He put me on the bench and left me there. However, because I was one of the Divine Ryans, he did not cut me from the team. So it was that I had become that unheard-of luxury, the third goalie. We were the only minor-league team in the city, perhaps in the world, that had three goalies. During games, I sat in the stands, in my civvies, because there was no room for me on the bench. "Draper Doyle, plain-clothes goalie," Uncle Reginald called me. Other times, it was "Draper Doyle, undercover goalie." The only time I had even got to sit in the dressing room with the other boys was before practice.

Some practice. After I practised putting on my equipment, I
practised sitting on the bench. Afterwards, I would walk home,
still wearing my equipment, my skates slung over my shoulder.
"Another gruelling practice?" Uncle Reginald said. I was to
have been the third goalie again this year. Not that my chances
of actually playing would have been any better. What, for instance, were the chances of both our goalies falling into such a
slump that to put me in the net would help the team? It must
have been when man was first faced with such calculations that
exponential numbers were invented. Despite the fact that to
avoid getting hit was the whole point of boxing, I doubted that
I would be much better at it. No doubt my vaunted puck-
dodging reflexes would fail me when punches were coming
at me instead. Because it now seemed to be mocking me, I took
"Draper Doyle: Goalie" down from the wall, rolled it up, and
put it in the closet.

I wondered if we would have to live with Aunt Phil forever.
It seemed likely, given what my mother earned, working at
Reg Ryan's. Aunt Phil took the cost of our room and board out
of my mother's salary, paying her only what little was left. We
each had our own rooms, which, along with Aunt Phil's, were
on the second floor. At least one empty room lay between each
bedroom and the next, and our mother's was at the far end of
the hall, so that it was quite easy for her to avoid Mary and me,
something she had become quite adept at doing. I had grown
used to seeing her for hardly more than an hour a day, at mealtimes, after which, once the dishes were done, she would make
some excuse about feeling tired and go to her room. She was
like some secret in the house, everyone avoiding mention of
her, or else talking darkly about her, about how poorly she
looked, how little she ate. Even had she not gone to her room
before the rest of us, we would have had little more than a
couple of hours with her, for she and Aunt Phil had to get up

at the absurd hour of five in the morning to prepare Reg Ryan's for the mourners, who started arriving as early as eight a.m.

Mary and I did not much like the idea of our mother working at Reg Ryan's. "Them that have no husbands must do what they can," Aunt Phil told us, looking disappointed when our mother did not chime in with some grim observation of her own. "Them that have no husbands..." "Them that are left behind...." She kept coming up with such phrases, looking at our mother as if she believed there must be some way of defining widowhood that would appeal to her. Our mother assured us that she had nothing to do with the actual undertaking at Reg Ryan's—nor, for that matter, did Aunt Phil. That was all taken care of by some man not related to the Ryans, a man whose identity, like that of the country's executioner, seemed to be a secret. By day, my mother and Aunt Phil were managers, working in the office on the top floor; by night, they were cleaning ladies, working below in the blue room and the red room. After all the mourners had left, they did the vacuuming, the polishing. She said they took turns polishing the caskets.

Before she died, Uncle Reginald's wife, Aunt Delia, had shared the work with them. "The Three Weird Sisters-in-law," Uncle Reginald had called them. He had somehow talked the three of them into posing for a photograph which he still displayed prominently on his mantelpiece. It was one of Uncle Reginald's prized possessions, that photograph. There they were, the Three Weird Sisters-in-law, standing like the forward line of some famous hockey team, but holding brooms instead of hockey sticks, Aunt Phil in the middle, our mother and Aunt Delia on either side of her. How he had convinced Aunt Phil and Aunt Delia, who in the photograph looked grimly serious, to crouch over their brooms like that was a mystery. What on earth had they imagined they were doing? Only our mother was smiling, smiling in a way that suggested some complicity on her part in getting the two older women to go along with it.

There was a faint series of knocks on my door. "Come in," I said. The door opened and Mary, wearing her slippers and pyjamas, scuffed into the room.

"Thanks for taking my side against Aunt Phil," I said. "You were a big help."

"I was only joking, Draper Doyle," she said.

"Some joke," I said. "What do you want?"

"Just don't wake up screaming tonight, OK, Draper Doyle?" she said. "Just don't wake up screaming." Many times, in the months since my father's death, I had woken screaming from nightmares which I could not remember. Even with their doors closed, the others could hear me. It had gotten so that Mary, who was in the room closest to mine, hated to go to sleep for fear of being wakened by my screaming. The only thing worse, she said, than having a nightmare, was hearing someone else have one.

"I can't help what dreams I have," I said.

For a while, she said nothing. Then she sat down on my bed. "Draper Doyle?" she said. I looked up. Lately, whenever I saw her with that solemn I-am-the-oldest-child-of-a-fatherless-family expression on her face, I ran the other way, for I knew that she wanted to talk about something. That is, she wanted to have one of those earnest conversations which she seemed to think people in other families were having all the time. It might have been that all over the city, while we Ryans were wasting time reading books or watching television, other families were sitting about, frankly admitting their real opinions of one another.

"This family never talks," she said. I rolled my eyes.

"Well we don't," she said. I tried to think of a way to head her off.

"I know you're worried about Mom," she said. It was always easy to know what was bothering Mary. It was whatever she claimed to think was bothering you.

"Maybe we should go in and see her," she said. Ever since our father had died, Mary was always suggesting that the two of us go in to "see" our mother, "to help her face up to it," she said. With the two of us helping her face up to it, it was never long before we had her crying. I didn't feel much like doing it again.

"C'mon," she said, "let's go in to see her." I shook my head.

"Why not?" she said.

"Because I don't feel like it," I said. She would never leave before I had either agreed to go with her or had said something so callous that she could feel entirely justified in giving up on me. I had hoped that "because I don't feel like it" would convince her that I was beyond hope, but it didn't.

"Draper Doyle?" she said. I looked up again to find that she was crying. She was doing nothing to hide the fact, not even wiping the tears as they ran down her face.

"You didn't really see him, did you?" she said. I nodded.

"Look, you didn't," she said. "So don't pretend you did, OK? And especially don't say it when Mom is around, OK? She's just getting over it, she doesn't want you—" She was crying so hard now that she stopped talking and put her hands over her face. Her shoulders were shaking. Considering what announcing my father's ghost had so far gotten me, I was only too glad to promise not to mention him again.

"All right," I said. "All right. I won't do it any more."

3

D ESPITE THE fact that Uncle Reginald was not involved in the actual running of Reg Ryan's, the popular notion was that, as had been true of his father Reg Ryan Sr. in the forties and fifties, he was the real brains behind it. "The power behind the crone," he called himself, the crone being Aunt Phil, who really ran things. The Divine Ryans did everything they could to keep alive this notion of Uncle Reginald as owner and proprietor—when it came to death, Aunt Phil said, people preferred to think that a man was in charge.

The truth was that Uncle Reginald was more of a symbol, more of a figurehead than anything else, "like Colonel Sanders," he said, though it was not a comparison that pleased Aunt Phil. His only official duty, for which he received, not the percentage of profits he was always asking for, but what he called a "piddling" salary, was to dress up in his black top-hat and waistcoat and drive the hearse, not only in funerals, but to make what were called "collections"—that is, to go to homes or to hospitals, to collect what Aunt Phil called "the customer" and bring them back to Reg Ryan's. Uncle Reginald did not do the actual collecting, but waited behind the wheel of the hearse, his hat removed, while it was done. He also ran whatever errands needed running, staying at home and waiting for one of the Weird Sisters-in-law to call him. He described himself as a combination of chauffeur and gopher, a "gauffeur" you might say.

To Aunt Phil, Sister Louise, and Father Seymour, Uncle Reginald was the embodiment of all that was wrong with Reg Ryan's. They were forever harking back to the old days, when horses were still used to draw the casket and Reg Ryan Sr. was still driving them. Were funerals better or worse now that horses were no longer used to pull the casket? This question, "the horse/hearse controversy," as Uncle Reginald called it, had been raging in the family for the past twenty years. At least the horses had known the way to the graveyard, Sister Louise was fond of pointing out, adding that that was more than you could say for Uncle Reginald. This was in reference to the fact that once, on the way to one of the more remote graveyards in the city, Uncle Reginald had taken a wrong turn. He had not been aware of it until one of the mourners, who had circled around to intercept him, flagged him down, and then, just to be sure, rode with him the rest of the way.

It had happened only that once, but Sister Louise would not let him forget it. "I shudder to think," she said, "where one of our funerals might end up some day."

While Uncle Reginald admitted that a horse had a better sense of direction than either a hearse or, in that one case, the person driving it, he personally found a hearse a lot easier to "operate." It had been one of his greatest fears, he said, during those few years that he had driven the horses, that he would lose control of them, and the funeral would go tearing like some runaway stagecoach through the streets. Well, said Sister Louise, the chance of his losing control of the hearse was just as great, if not greater, given that he had no driver's licence, in fact refused to get one. Uncle Reginald pointed out that, since the only car he drove was the hearse, it was extremely unlikely that he would ever be asked to show his licence. "It doesn't matter," said Sister Louise. "You should have one." "Well let me put it this way," said Uncle Reginald. "Were I to try to get one now, the whole world would find out that, for the past twenty years, I didn't have one." That it was out of the question for him to get his licence at this point, Sister Louise begrudgingly admitted, but she said his not having one was a "shameful impropriety" that he would one day have to answer for.

Some years back, when, like ours, their house had been sold for the greater good—that is, tossed into the great black maw of *The Daily Chronicle* which, only a short time later, was hungry for more—Aunt Delia and Uncle Reginald had moved in with Aunt Phil. Uncle Reginald had opposed the move, but Aunt Phil had threatened to have him evicted, "brother or no brother," as she put it. They did not actually live with Aunt Phil, but had a large, self-contained apartment on the upper floor, to which you could climb, from the outside by way of the fire-escape, and from the inside by way of a kind of warehouse lift which they had had installed. Uncle Reginald, who now lived in the apartment by himself, loved using the lift, often descending unannounced to visit us. "To stir up trouble," Aunt Phil said.

The first sign that he was on his way would be a whirring sound from above, then the squeaking of the cables as the lift came down through what was once a stairwell at the end of the hall. The devil *ex machina* Uncle Reginald called the lift, further exasperating Aunt Phil by refusing to explain to anyone what this meant. Uncle Reginald usually went out by way of the fire-escape and, to avoid climbing the stairs, came in by way of the lift. However, when he was heading out to a funeral, Aunt Phil had him use the lift, pointing out that it would not do for Reg Ryan to be seen in full costume "clomping" down four flights of stairs.

We always gathered at the lift to watch him appear. It was quite an impressive sight, Uncle Reginald descending slowly into view, dressed all in black, his spats appearing first, then his trousers, then his waistcoat and his top-hat which was so high that, upon stepping from the lift, he had to duck his head. To me, Uncle Reginald's height was a kind of physical manifestation of his oddness. Where such height had come from in a family that, as he put it, was "notoriously short," no one seemed to know. He described himself as "a shade over six feet tall," or sometimes as "a shade, over six feet tall," pausing just long enough after "shade" to make people wonder if the second meaning was intentional.

There was something regal about the way he held himself, a kind of mournful grace in the way he moved. He called himself "the most dapper Grim Reaper this side of the Atlantic." Sometimes we applauded, though this was often cut short by Aunt Phil, who would give him the onceover, making sure that nothing was amiss. It was all he could do to stand for this inspection, frowning straight ahead, as Aunt Phil, like some drill sergeant, walked around him, now and then picking bits of lint from his uniform. When she was through, he would straighten up and adjust his top-hat to the proper angle. "Another ferry to the mainland," he'd say. Then Aunt Phil would take his arm and escort him to the hearse, which was parked in the backyard where no one in the neighbourhood could see it. When she had more or less installed him in the hearse and he was headed up the street towards Reg Ryan's, she would wait at the end of the driveway, keeping an eye out until the procession, led by Uncle Reginald, left the funeral home.

Because in the mornings our mother and Aunt Phil were at Reg Ryan's, it was left to Uncle Reginald to get us ready for school, which he managed to do without even coming down from his apartment. He got us out of bed by sending the empty lift up and down until we woke up and screamed for him to stop. Then, while we were getting washed and dressed, he cooked our breakfast, sending it down on the lift, dumbwaiter style. He never showed himself, never said a word, even if we complained about how something was prepared. Every morning, he made sure to forget at least one thing. "You forgot the milk," I'd shout. Minutes later, down, all by itself on the lift, would come a glass of milk. Sometimes, the entire cargo of the lift was one lump of sugar, descending ceremoniously in the middle of a plate.

We couldn't get such things from the downstairs kitchen because it was locked, Aunt Phil not trusting even twelve-year-old Mary to work the stove properly. For the same reason, we ate breakfast in the dining room, Mary and I, just the two of us at that huge table. Every morning, we stood at the bottom of the lift, waiting for our breakfast to appear like manna from above, then carried our trays to the dining room, where, subdued by the room and by the prospect of another day at school, we ate in silence. Before leaving, we put our trays on the lift and watched them rise slowly out of sight.

Aunt Phil's, or rather, Reg Ryan Sr.'s dining room, was hung with the kind of portraits you could otherwise only see in low-budget horror films, a gallery of grandfathers looking down at you as you ate, staring at you, Uncle Reginald said, as if they hoped their very expressions would make you choke on your food. Uncle Reginald called them "our four fathers" and swore that their portraits were intended to stir the family into action, to shame us into preserving what they had handed down to us, and for which they had obviously suffered much. Grandpa Stern, Grandpa Cross, Grandpa Grim, and Grandpa Disapproving, he called them. They were, in fact, his great-great-grandfather, his great-grandfather, his grandfather, and his father, representing, he said, one hundred years in the newspaper publishing and undertaking businesses, one hundred years of digging up dirt of one kind or another.

Grandpa Stern had been the first New World undertaker in the family, the art of undertaking having been practised by the

Old World side of the family since the early 1700s. At least according to Aunt Phil. Uncle Reginald swore that the Old World Ryans had only been gravediggers. Still, he told me, I came from a long line of undertakers, and might end up one myself if I wasn't careful. It might be in my blood after all, he said, telling me that the first indication of being a born undertaker would be an urge to rearrange the features of people who were sleeping. If I should ever find myself creeping out of bed to turn up the corners of Mary's mouth into a smile, he said, I should let him know at once. I told him that newspapers might be more my line. He grimaced. "Worse again," he said. "You're better off undertaking. It's less morbid."

Grandpa Cross, his great-grandfather, had started *The Daily Chronicle*, then called *The Daily Catholic Chronicle*. His grandfather, Grandpa Grim, otherwise known as Patrick Ryan, had seen *The Daily Chronicle* through its heyday. Under his guidance, as well as that of his two brothers, the *Chronicle* ruined the careers of many a Protestant politician, prompting someone at the time to observe that, while one side of the Ryan family buried Catholics, the other buried Protestants. Grandpa Disapproving, his father, Reg Ryan Sr., who had seen fit to give Uncle Reginald his name, but not one cent of his money or one inch of his real estate, was pictured in his undertaker's outfit, identical to the one Uncle Reginald wore, except, as Uncle Reginald never tired of pointing out, about six sizes smaller. Reg Ryan Sr. looked faintly absurd in the outfit—of all the things people imagined death to be, said Uncle Reginald, five foot six and badly overweight were not among them. Reg Ryan Sr. had not only run the funeral home, but had been the publisher and editor of the *Chronicle*, working himself to death by the age of fifty-two, his reward for which, said Uncle Reginald, was a free wake in his own funeral home and a free obituary in his own newspaper.

"Worked himself to death," Aunt Phil said, more boastfully than otherwise.

✦

One morning, while I was having breakfast in the dining room, I heard the lift descend and, thinking some special treat might be waiting for me, went to investigate. On the floor of the lift was a round silver tray, and on the tray an envelope marked "Draper Doyle." I picked up the envelope and, looking inside, found a note which read, "Come see me after school. Use the fire-escape." That afternoon, I climbed the fire-escape stairs and knocked on Uncle Reginald's door. He let me into his apartment which looked as if the very walls were made of books. Books were scattered everywhere, on the window ledge, on the floor. Uncle Reginald had to clear a space on the sofa so I could sit down. He asked me if I had seen my father's ghost lately. I told him my father had last appeared to me two nights ago, this time in what had been our backyard, where he had stood tossing a puck in the air and watching with apparent fascination as it fell to the ground. Over and over he had done it, thrown the puck so that it fluttered end over end, high in the air, then watched it fall to earth. By the time I ran downstairs and out the door, the backyard was empty. I had searched the grass in case he had left the puck behind, but hadn't found it.

Uncle Reginald nodded, then had me sit in an armchair opposite his. He asked me if I had ever heard of psycho-oralysis. I made a face and shook my head. It was, he said, the opposite of psychoanalysis. He told me that the job of an analyst was to listen, while the job of an oralyst was to speak. The job of an analyst was to take his patient seriously. The job of an oralyst was to make him laugh. An analyst had his patient lie on a couch. An oralyst had him tell the truth, whether it was on a couch or somewhere else—only the oralyst was allowed to lie, which he could be counted on to do almost constantly. The analyst spoke of nothing but the patient's problems. The oralyst went off on tangents entirely irrelevant to the patient's problems, in fact did so as often as possible, thereby confusing the patient and having fun at his expense.

The analyst sat out of sight of the patient who did all the talking—the patient, in other words, was treated like an adult, his desire for privacy respected. He was heard but never seen. With the oralyst, the patient was seen but never heard—in other words, treated like a child, which was entirely appropriate, Uncle Reginald said, since I happened to be one. In psychoanalysis, there was something called "free association." In psycho-oralysis, there was fee association, a technique by which every word spoken by the oralyst reminded the patient of how much money this was costing him.

"Which brings me," said Uncle Reginald, "to the question of my fee."

"Your fee?" I said.

"My fee," he said. "Oralysis will do you no good whatsoever unless you have to pay for it. How does one session a week, fifty cents per session sound?"

"That's half my allowance," I said. He shrugged.

I tried to get him to explain more clearly exactly what psycho-oralysis was, but he assured me that I now knew as much about it as he did.

"Fifty cents," I said. "Will it do me any good?"

"You should consider yourself lucky," he said. "Hamlet, who also saw his father's ghost, did not have nearly so nice an uncle."

We agreed that on Tuesday afternoons, the one afternoon a week I had free from practice for Father Seymour's Number, I would come to see him, to be oralyzed. He told me that, for

our sessions, I should never use the lift. Using the outside entrance, climbing the fire-escape, would make things seem more
official, he said, more like we were strangers, patient and oralyst. "But for God's sake," he said, "don't tell anyone you're
being oralyzed by your uncle. If you do, I'll be arrested." Though
I asked him, he refused to explain what he meant by this.

How I began to look forward to plodding up those steps, a
nine-year-old in need of therapy, my lunchbox in my hand, my
schoolbag bouncing. There to be oralyzed by Uncle Reginald,
who, I now realize, was quite right in not wanting me to use
that phrase in public.

They became the highlight of my week, those secret sessions
with Uncle Reginald. Our first concerned tap-dancing. I lay on
Uncle Reginald's couch and listened while he held forth on the
matter. He began by defining tap-dancing as "the art of making
an irritating sound with one's feet." What, he asked me—
rhetorically, for I was not allowed to speak—what was the point
of spending half your life perfecting a skill that no one else
could stand to see performed? Everyone hated tap-dancing.
Everyone hated those absurdly clicking shoes, not to mention
the dancer, going about the stage with that eager-to-please
expression on his face, swinging his arms, and making those
barely perceptible movements with his feet. The sound must be
exactly right, Father Seymour always said, for it was the sound
that people paid attention to—it was in the sound that one's
mistakes were most obvious, most glaring. But there was something inherently wrong, Uncle Reginald said, with a dance that
you did not so much watch as listen to.

Our second session concerned Sister Louise. What had fascinated all of them when they were children, Uncle Reginald
said, was that in one millimetre of skin, Sister Louise had total
feeling, and in the next none at all. When she walked her
fingers down her body, she simply stopped feeling them at her

waist. It was as though she was walking her fingers on a mirror when, suddenly, their reflection disappeared. One day, he said, they tried to pin down the exact point where the feeling stopped. They had her lie on the bed with her blouse pulled up and, while she stared at the ceiling, Aunt Phil and Uncle Reginald bent over her like surgeons. Aunt Phil, touching her belly with the blunt end of a knitting needle, found a spot, then had Uncle Reginald mark it with a pen. When there was a row of dots across her stomach, they turned her over and did the other side, dotting her back with the pen. In the end, Sister Louise was wearing a girdle of blue dots, which Uncle Reginald then joined together to form what he decided would be called "the paraline," below which she felt nothing.

The paraline. I tried to imagine Sister Louise ever having been so young, so girlish as to go along with such a thing. The very thought of her having a belly, let alone letting someone write on it, seemed preposterous. The only parts of her body I had ever seen were her hands and her face. I had never seen her hair. I could easily have been convinced that she didn't have any. Nor could I imagine any sort of body lying beneath the black folds of her habit. All I ever saw of her legs was her black boots on the footrest of the wheelchair. Those massive black boots—it might have been those boots that confined her to the chair, so solid, so heavy did they seem. She never wheeled herself about, there being always far more volunteers for this task than were necessary. Instead of asking for help, she would drop her prayer beads in her lap and make as if to put her hands on the wheels. She never failed to seem surprised when half the people present came running to stop her. She had a way of sitting in the chair that made you forget that she was paralyzed and made you think that it was simply her preferred form of travel, or that it was a kind of regal eccentricity of hers, a kind of mobile throne.

The notion of the paraline stayed with me. I wondered if such a line might separate this world from the next. Death might be nothing more than a slight shift in the paraline. A slight shift back the other way, and someone I saw waked last week is coming up the steps. A slight shift was all it would take to get me, I suspected, given how close to the paraline I must be to be seeing my father's ghost so often. I was barely onside, so to speak, like Beliveau in full flight, crouching for a pass at the blueline, his upper body well inside the line, while his skates were still outside.

One night, I dreamed that I was paralzyed, confined to a wheelchair in which I was gliding on the ice at the Montreal Forum without so much as touching the wheels. Then I was standing, still gliding effortlessly, but on a pair of skates. I was still paralyzed, for I could not feel my legs, though I could see them. I knew that it was only by looking at them that I could invest them with the power to hold me upright. I knew that if I looked away, I would fall.

Then fog began to rise from the Forum ice, slowly at first, swirling about my feet, obscuring my skates, then rising quickly to my knees, then to my thighs. Finally, there was a circle of sensation at my waist, as though I were being immersed in cold water; this circle of sensation climbed up my body as each successive inch of me first felt the fog, then stopped feeling it. It was as though, inch by inch, I was being erased. When it reached my neck, I tipped my head back and began to scream. I woke up and, for the first time since my father's death, remembered the nightmare. It didn't seem like progress of any kind, given that the dream now had the power of scaring me while I was still awake.

4

———

THOUGH MY membership in Father Seymour's Number turned out to be every bit as time-consuming as I had expected, it was far less demanding, mostly because, as I soon discovered, I was a member in name only. Right from the start, Father Seymour seemed to regret having accepted me into his Number. Each boy in Father Seymour's Number engaged in two of the three disciplines—mine, he said, would be boxing and singing, since he doubted, from what he had heard about the way I played goal, that I could ever learn to dance. It was possible, he said, that since I played goal like someone who was not wearing goalie pads, I might tap-dance like someone who was.

As for the boxing, it was soon evident that he was afraid to let me box for fear of what my mother would think if I went home with both eyes blackened. He told me that, since there was no chance that I would be good enough by next March to take part in the tournament, he would take his time bringing me along. (The boxing tournament came a couple of months after the Christmas concert, which made sense when you thought about it. It wouldn't have done for the members of a choir to look all beaten up while singing "Ave Maria," or to have black eyes while dancing.) It might be best, he said, if I simply used the time until Christmas to get in shape and to "observe" the other boys, at which point he would find me a sparring partner. I spent each afternoon wandering more or less unsupervised about the gym, doing laps and pushups with the other boys but never sparring with them, "observing" them as they boxed.

Even in the gym, Father Seymour dressed in black, black undershirt, black shorts, black socks and sneaker boots. It was strange to see him in such an outfit, with his chest and his arms and legs showing, covered in hair that was so black it might have been part of his habit, some basic layer that covered his whole body, even those parts still hidden by his clothes. He walked about the gym, going from one pair of boxers to another, telling them what mistakes they were making, exhorting them to work harder. "C'mon boys," he roared. "We fight United in the spring. We better be ready."

He was always on the lookout for boys who were not practising or were otherwise misbehaving. There were frequent strappings, and always an embarrassing, somehow shameful interval while Father Seymour unlaced the boxing gloves of the boy he was about to strap. The boy would stand there, holding out his gloves for Father Seymour to unlace, Father Seymour doing so quite calmly, as if being strapped was just a routine part of learning how to box. So close in height was he to some of the boys, he had to rise up on his toes to strap them properly, rise up to increase the distance the strap had to travel before it hit their hand. He rose with each blow, up on his toes, then down again, the sound of grit beneath his boots always just preceding the sound of the strap hitting the boy's hand. He always maintained a kind of joviality with the boy whom he was strapping, as if the whole thing was somehow inevitable, a kind of time-honoured tradition that he and the boy were acting out, as if it was part of a boy's essential nature to be strapped, and part of a priest's to do the strapping. He seemed to admire especially those boys who took their punishment in this spirit, regarding the strap, their stinging hands with a kind of wry amusement.

After he had finished strapping them, he was always quite solici-
tous, helping them put their stinging hands back into their
boxing gloves, then, just as slowly and calmly as he had unlaced
them, lacing them up again.

He spent most of his time with the older boys, teaching
them how to move, how to throw and block punches. The
younger boys, the boys from age ten down, he left more or
less to themselves, so that they engaged in furious, if unskilled
slugging fests all afternoon, running back and forth from the
bathroom with bloody noses. I was advised to pay special attention to one of these younger boys, to "observe" him especially
closely. Unlike the other boys his age, he boxed instead of
brawled; in fact, he boxed, and quite routinely defeated, boys
who were years older than he was. The boy whom Father
Seymour referred to as Young Leonard was the star of the
Number. He was the only boy in Father Seymour's Number
allowed to train in all three disciplines. Father Seymour was
always pointing to Young Leonard, making him an example for
the rest of us.

Not only was Young Leonard the best boxer and the best
dancer, but he was one of only four soloists in the choir. Unlike
many of the others, he looked like a choirboy. When I first
saw him, I doubted that he could dance, let alone box, so thin
were his arms and legs. His boxing gloves looked like great
weights that someone had attached to him to keep his arms forever at his sides. It was obvious that Young Leonard thought
very little of someone who had not earned his way into Father
Seymour's Number. "So you're half an orphan," he said. I realized that Father Seymour must have repeated Mary's joke. "An
orphan from the waist down," he said, "or from the waist up?"
I felt like telling him that, given his height, it might be more
appropriate to say that *he* was half an orphan, but I thought better of it.

When it came to singing, it was not so easy for Father Seymour to get me out of his hair. The problem was the promise he had made to my mother to have me in the chorus by Christmas. He gave me the standard audition he gave would-be members of Father Seymour's Number, then informed me that I had failed it miserably. He assured me that I would do far more damage with my singing than with my boxing—as much as I might dread sparring with Young Leonard, so would Young Leonard dread singing with me. Perhaps, he said, instead of swinging at my sparring partner after Christmas, I should try singing at him, putting him down for the count with a combination of shrieking off-key notes. I tried to imagine it, Young Leonard, his ears covered with his boxing gloves, fleeing from me as I chased him round the gym singing "Ave Maria" more horribly than it was ever sung before. "Remember," Father Seymour said, "when the bell rings, come out singing." The other boys roared with laughter.

It soon became apparent that I would not be ready even to sing in the chorus by the time of the Christmas concert. On top of that, he said, my voice would throw off the others. Perhaps it would be best if I no longer practised with the choir. I could practise on my own, he said, and he would help me, when he had the time. He made me promise not to tell my mother or Aunt Phil about it. I was more than happy to oblige. I'd have done anything to get out of choir practice. I had to continue to attend, he said, so that neither my mother nor Aunt Phil would wonder why I was coming home from school so early, but I no longer had to sing.

Each afternoon, I went to the hall, and Father Seymour had me sit down at the back where, as he put it, I could make myself useful. My usefulness consisted of answering yes or no when asked if I could hear properly what the other boys were singing. This should be their goal, he told them, to make themselves heard to Draper Doyle. Could I make out the words? he asked me. When I assured him I could, he would have me recite them back to him. "Sad are the men of Nottingham," I said, my voice echoing throughout the hall. "Sad are they who toil for the king."

5

─────

I HAD PUT together, from half-heard playground conversations, an almost accurate version of what I had once heard
Sister Louise refer to as "the sex act." I believed that the man
put his pee-swollen bud inside the woman—that is, up her
backside, there being, so far as I knew, no other place to put
it—then did his pee, the unlikely result of which was that the
woman had a baby some time later.

"He's free now," Aunt Phil had told my mother one day as
we were walking home from the cemetery. "Free from the
marriage bed." Though I was fairly sure I knew, I asked Uncle
Reginald what Aunt Phil meant by "the marriage bed."

"The beast with two backs," said Uncle Reginald.

"The what?" I said.

"The beast with two backs," he said. "Older than the dino-
saurs. Not yet extinct." He seemed surprised when I nodded to
indicate that I understood what he meant, but he said nothing.

The beast with two backs. That seemed a good way of
putting it. I looked up "beast" in the dictionary. One of the
definitions was "a human being swayed by animal propensities."

"Do you know what you are?" Uncle Reginald asked me
that same day during oralysis.

"What do you mean?" I said.

"You my boy," he said, "are the future of the family. The
only boy that this generation of Ryans has produced. Or will
produce, now that your father is gone. There would be no
more Ryans if not for you."

This fact, which had never occurred to me before, made me feel very uneasy. The awfulness of the sex act was one of the few things about which Aunt Phil and I agreed, though she, of course, would have been shocked to know that I had even heard of the sex act, let alone that I shared her opinion of it.

My father and Uncle Reginald were what Aunt Phil called "the laymen of the family." Laymen were as rare among the Ryans as priests were among other families. Aunt Phil talked as if, for a man, marriage was the supreme sacrifice. While becoming a priest did not appeal to me, I could certainly see the advantages of celibacy. Never mind Father Seymour, never mind Father Francis, braving the jungles of South America to bring religion to the natives — it was my father and Uncle Reginald, who had braved the horrors of the marriage bed to keep the family name going, who were the real missionaries of the family.

The Ryans had disapproved of my parents having only two children. I didn't know if either my mother or my father had ever been taken aside and spoken to about it, but Aunt Phil had often made passing reference to it. Any mention of the attractiveness of my mother's figure had drawn from Aunt Phil the observation that a figure was all very well, but having children was more important. It was the same if someone remarked at our mother's ability to hold down a full-time job while raising a family. "A family?" Aunt Phil said. "Is that what two children are being called nowadays?"

Still, as much as Aunt Phil believed that child-bearing was one of the sacramental duties of marriage, she always looked at children with a kind of grimace of disgust. I suspected that one of Aunt Phil's objections to children was that they were visible proof that their parents had had sex, and were therefore an embarrassment to everyone. It was an objection I could well understand, given the nature of that hilarious indignity known as "the sex act." A couple walking down the street with five children were publicly flaunting the fact that they had done it five times. Each innocent little toddler, done up in his sailor suit and knee socks, might as well have been a photograph of his parents doing it, for the way that Aunt Phil looked at him.

No wonder she and Father Seymour had such a fondness for orphans. At least they never appeared in public with their parents. In fact, you could easily pretend that they had no parents—that is, that they had never had them. Young Leonard and the others were not of woman born, it seemed. "Aren't they just divine," people said, when they appeared on stage in their green jackets and their buckled shoes. "A horde of little divinities," Uncle Reginald called them. "Orphans are the children of God," Aunt Phil said, making me wonder just how literally she meant it.

I had once asked her where babies came from. Fumbling for words, she had blurted out, "They come from God," and then, upon being further pressed, had said that people "ordered" them through their parish priest. She had ever since been forced to stick with this answer, reluctantly repeating it whenever I asked. Finally, she forbade me to ask her anymore, so Uncle Reginald had taken it up, asking her "Where do babies come from, Aunt Phil?" at which Aunt Phil would only glare at him. Uncle Reginald said that everyone had heard of Charles Darwin's *Origin of Species*, the book which had overthrown religion as it was known, but how many had heard of Philomena Ryan's *Origin of Babies*, the book which had overthrown science as it was known?

I knew that the "sex act" had to do also with original sin, which my father had told me I should think of as the crime in a game of Clue. "If the crime was original sin," my father said, "the solution would be: 'The woman. In the garden. With the apple.'" The woman, I took this to mean, had—though God only knew how—tempted the man to put his pee-swollen bud into her backside. A crime, it seemed to me, if there ever was one.

Although I had never seen any female completely naked, I had seen two females half naked, my mother from the waist up and Mary from the waist down. I had seen my mother one night, a few months before my father died, quite by accident. Thinking I had heard someone crying, I had gotten out of bed and was headed down the hallway when I realized that the sound was coming, not from Mary's room, as I had suspected, but from my parents', the door of which was slightly open. At first, all I saw was that, sitting up in bed, my mother was holding my father, rocking him gently back and forth. My father, crying in my mother's arms.

Then I noticed that the top of her nightgown was open, and that he was at her breast, his mouth moving slowly. There was a kind of forlorn pleading in the tenderness with which she held him, as well as in his crying. What a strange sight it was, my father sniffling, suckling, doing both at exactly the same time, his hands folded at his waist as if no part of him must touch her but his mouth. When he pulled away and rolled over on his side, my mother, too, rolled over on her side, but, for an instant, both her breasts, her soft, pink-nippled breasts, had been revealed to me.

I had gotten a look at Mary by the time-honoured method of peeking through the keyhole at her on one of the rare occasions when she forgot to hang a towel on the doorknob while undressing. This, too, had been but a few months ago. My first reaction had been a fit of giggles, for I presumed the hair between her legs, which looked like a beard, was some absurdity peculiar to females. Wasn't it just like a girl to have a big ball of fur between her legs?

Though it meant confessing to peeping at Mary, I couldn't resist bringing it up the next time we were having dinner.

"Mary, Mary, bum so hairy, how do you make it grow?" I said, which sent Mary running to her room. My mother had brought me back to earth by assuring me that "Men have hair there, too."

One half of my mother, one half of Mary, made up the sum total of my knowledge of female anatomy. Now, a few months after I had first seen them, and always on those nights when I had seen my father's ghost, a woman consisting of these two halves sewn together began appearing in my dreams. Half Mom, half Mary—"Momary," I called her. She was thirty-five years old above the waist and twelve years old below it. I remember the weird disproportion of the halves, my mother's big-breasted torso waddling about on Mary's skinny legs. Even worse was the fact that the two halves were joined by a dotted line like the one Uncle Reginald had drawn around Sister Louise. No matter how hard I tried, I could not imagine Momary without that dotted line, the paraline, let alone dream her without it.

Top-heavy, sewn together, her stitching plainly visible, as well as with what I still thought of as a beard between her legs, Momary pursued me through my nightmares, asking only for a kiss, but blinking her eyes in a kind of mock rapture which suggested she might want much more. Each time, the nightmare ended, not with a kiss, but with sudden darkness, or rather the sensation of being accelerated through total darkness, moving at some impossible velocity through space so empty that even my own body was invisible.

One morning, I woke from the Momary dream to find myself in mid-pee. My underwear was soaked and I only just managed to stop before I stained the sheets. I ran to the bathroom, my bud so hard I had to pee while standing on the bathtub. When I was finished, I took my underwear and threw it in the laundry. About a week later, it happened again. I dreamed that, in fleeing from Momary, I ran headlong into darkness so absolute, so silent that I doubted my existence, then woke up to find myself in mid-pee. Once again, I put a pair of pee-stained drawers in the laundry.

To explain why Aunt Phil did what she did with my underwear, I have to tell first what Mary and my mother did with hers. Mary had recently disappointed Aunt Phil by developing breasts. "Twelve years old," Aunt Phil said, shaking her head and looking at my mother as if to say "What kind of woman would allow her daughter to have breasts at age twelve?" No one was more embarrassed by it all than Mary, though she pretended not to be. Rather than avoiding all mention of the topic, as she might have been expected to do, she went out of her way to mention it, to be mature about it, mortifying Aunt Phil and my mother in the process. Then, one afternoon, while Aunt Phil was out, Mary, who, for the past month, had been assuring everyone that breasts were not something to make jokes about or be ashamed of, came up from the basement wearing Aunt Phil's bra outside her sweater, the cups of the bra stuffed, as Mary put it, with "most" of that week's laundry. "Look what I found," she said. "Aunt Phil left the laundry door unlocked."

It might have been that all the awkwardness and embarrassment that Mary had been storing up for weeks were in that bra, as if her breasts had become so absurdly oversized that she would have no choice but be embarrassed by them. My mother shrieked with laughter when she saw her, causing Mary to laugh even harder and strut around the kitchen with her chest thrust out. Her face was beet red with a kind of mortified hilarity which increased the more my mother laughed at her. There they were, the legendary bras which Aunt Phil would not even hang on the clothesline for fear of people seeing them.

Then my mother ran down to the basement and came back with another of Aunt Phil's bras, the cups of which, as she discovered, fit quite nicely on her head, looking like a bathing cap, or like one of those caps pilots wore in World War II, all the more so when she fastened the straps beneath her chin. My mother walked about the kitchen as if she was modelling the latest thing in aviation hats, turning her head this way and that. Soon, all three of us were in the giggles.

Then, she ran downstairs again and, seconds later, came back up, still wearing Aunt Phil's bra, but also wearing—it hardly seemed possible—Father Seymour's underwear, "the sacred shorts" as Uncle Reginald called them, which Father Seymour delivered to Aunt Phil cloak-and-dagger fashion every Friday. The rest of his laundry was done by the sisters at the convent, but the shorts were withheld. And here was my mother, wearing them on her head, wearing them over Aunt Phil's bra, the cups of which, doubled on her head, looked like a skullcap. She might have been some court jester, some fool figure, for, with the skullcap bra, and the shorts, the legs of which hung drooping down like tassels, the only thing missing was a set of bells.

By this time, tears were streaming down our faces—had it gone on much longer, all three of us might have fallen to the floor. But just when all the hilarity was at its height, Aunt Phil came through the door.

At first, it was only the riot of fun that she objected to, the noise that we were making. "My God," she said, taking off her bandanna, "I leave the house for half an hour—" And then she noticed them, her bras. Her sister-in-law was wearing one of them on her head, her niece was wearing the other one outside her sweater, while her nine-year-old nephew was watching them. It must have looked to her like some sort of pagan ritual was underway, some dance in celebration of the breasts.

For some reason, perhaps because her mind would simply not admit the possibility that my mother was wearing them on her head, it took her a little longer to notice, or perhaps to recognize, Father Seymour's shorts. She stared at my mother's head as if she could not, for the life of her, make out what she was wearing. My mother stood there, the legs of Father Seymour's shorts half drooping over so that now they looked like horns. Even with Aunt Phil looking at them in such total disbelief, Mary and my mother could not stop laughing. In fact, her being there made them laugh that much harder. "I'm going to leave this room for five minutes," Aunt Phil said. "I trust that when I come back, there will be no one in it."

It was hardly surprising, after all of this, which happened just before my second pee-dream, that I came home a few days after that dream to find that Aunt Phil had pinned my pee-stained underwear to the bulletin board in the kitchen. Because my drawers were otherwise lily white, the pee stain was all too evident. It might have been my little boy's soul that was hanging there, "pristine except for piss stains," as Uncle Reginald said later. Below the underwear was a note which read: "I will not wash such filth."

No sooner had I spotted my drawers than Aunt Phil took them down and threw them in the garbage. Worst of all was that no one said a word about it. Even Mary was too ashamed of me to gloat about the sight of my soiled underwear, hung on the board for all to see. The victory in the laundry had been undone. Aunt Phil had gotten her revenge. She had not only humiliated us, she had made us the instrument of our own humiliation. For a while, my mother and Mary blamed me as much as they did Aunt Phil, and no wonder, for they had had the worst of it; they had had to sit about the house while my underwear was on display in the kitchen. And no sooner had I arrived home than Aunt Phil had taken it down. I had been spared all but a momentary glimpse of it.

It was brilliant revenge, I had to give her that. Divide and conquer. And revenge, she must have calculated, that would keep us in line from now on, since it could well be repeated, my bladder being what it was. I had a picture of this scene being repeated ad infinitum, or, worse yet, the threat of its being repeated held over all our heads ad infinitum. The drawers wars. In which I had not fired a shot, but which we had started, so anything Aunt Phil did would seem justified. I couldn't help thinking that the sanctity of the laundry basket had been violated, first by us and now by her. It now seemed to me that anything found in the laundry basket, just like anything said in confession, should be kept strictly confidential, but it was too late for such pious thoughts. What if I peed again? As I well might, since I was almost certain to see my father again, and therefore to dream of Momary again.

I lay awake all that night thinking about it. What could I do? Any plan involving Mary or my mother would not be acceptable. I wanted to convince not only Aunt Phil, but the others as well, that I was not a bedwetter. I kept picturing Aunt Phil throwing my underwear in the garbage, and then it came to me. I would buy my own. I would throw my soiled underwear away and buy my own. I would need to buy one, at most two pairs of underwear a week. I had better start doing it right away, before my mother thought of doing the same thing for me. She was certain to replace the ones Aunt Phil had thrown away, and that might give her the idea. The thought of my mother having to buy me new underwear every week was enough to make me put aside such quibbles as where I would buy them, how I would raise the money (it was hard just scraping together enough for my oralysis), and how I would keep my secret from the others.

As I was lying there in bed, the same questions kept posing themselves to me, over and over. How had it come about that my family's happiness depended on my having clean underwear?

Did underwear play so large a part in the lives of other people? All of this trouble because of my bud, my "alarm cock," Uncle Reginald might have called it, if I had had the nerve to tell him why it kept going off, why it kept waking me up. I doubted that even Uncle Reginald would believe that my alarm cock went off to save me from the darkness that Momary chased me into once a week.

A few days later, after first seeing my father and later being awakened from yet another Momary dream by my alarm cock, to find myself in mid-pee, I took my allowance, which I had been saving since the kitchen episode, and went to the only Woolworth's within walking distance to buy my first pair of underwear. I will never forget the way the woman behind the counter looked at me. What kind of nine-year-old buys his own underwear? she was wondering. The kind who lives with Aunt Phil, I should have told her. Luckily, my mother bought only the standard Stanfield's whites, so I didn't have to go to any great lengths to find a matching pair.

As bad as that first time was, the second time, one week later, was much worse. The saleswoman had been so struck by a nine-year-old buying his own underwear that she remembered me, and smiled at me when I put the Stanfield's on the counter. I thought about telling her they were a present for my brother, but that would be hard to swallow, especially by the tenth week. Another brother, another birthday, another pair of Stanfield's whites, size small. Keeping the family in underwear and only nine years old. Probably not even wearing any himself, poor thing, going without for his brother's sake. I took the underwear and ran, wishing there was another Woolworth's within walking distance of our house.

✴

Thinking of that beard between Momary's legs, of which I was getting an ever closer view every night, got me to wondering why, despite my young age, the little sac between my legs was so weirdly wrinkled. At our next oralysis, I asked Uncle Reginald about it. He told me it was wrinkled because it was thousands of years old, being the only part of the human body which was passed down through generations, God giving to each newborn baby a "used Methuselah," shrunken, of course, to make it fit. "Methuselah," Uncle Reginald called it, the hairless, wrinkled sage between my legs. Though I did not believe his story, the thought of owning a used Methuselah fascinated me. I couldn't help wondering who had my father's, or Adam's for that matter. Imagine, going about with the very first Methuselah between your legs.

"The wisest of the wise," said Uncle Reginald. "The oracle of oracles. The centre of the world."

"My Methuselah is the centre of the world?" I said. He nodded.

"The centre of your world," he said. There was even an invocation to Methuselah, he said, to be spoken while looking at him, that is, while looking at his reflection in a mirror held between your legs. "Oh Methuselah," said Uncle Reginald, "oh Great Hairless One, Great Wrinkled One, oh Oracle of Oracles, oh Prune of Prunes, oh Wisest of the Wise, I command you, tell me all."

"He won't answer me," I said, rolling my eyes, but Uncle Reginald assured me that he would. Just for the fun of it, I began to make mock consultations with Methuselah whenever I took a bath. Sitting up on the edge of the tub, holding one of my mother's compact mirrors between my legs, I had Methuselah answer me, in a deep, god-like voice. "What is your question?" said Methuselah, when I recited Uncle Reginald's invocation.

"Will the Habs win the Stanley Cup this year?" I asked him.

"Yes," said Methuselah.

"Will Beliveau be MVP?" I said.

"Yes," said Methuselah. How strange he looked, my wizened, reincarnated Methuselah, how out of place between my backside and my bud, as if he had been some afterthought of creation, made in a panic and hastily attached at the last minute. Perhaps it was because he couldn't stand the sight of them that God had decided not to make any more Methuselahs than he absolutely had to, and to have mankind keep covered those he had made. It might have been no more than God's disgust with Adam's Methuselah that got our first parents kicked out of Eden.

I decided my Methuselah had once been Virgil's, my father's favourite writer, which made him at least two thousand years old. Between how many pairs of legs had he been stuck since then? I wondered. Who would have thought it, the accumulated wisdom of the ages in that little pouch between my legs? One day, while I was having a bath, I decided to ask him a real question. Sitting on the edge of the tub, I put the mirror between my legs and looked at him—with his many folds and pink wrinkles, he looked like a brain of some sort, a brain that stored the future instead of the past, foreknowledge instead of memory. "Oh Methuselah," I said, "oh Great Hairless One, Great Wrinkled One, oh Oracle of Oracles, oh Prune of Prunes, oh Wisest of the Wise, tell me all."

"What is your question?" said Methuselah.

"When will I see my father's ghost again?" I said.

"Soon," said Methuselah.

"When?" I said.

Methuselah, his pink wrinkles making him look like some aged child, said nothing.

"What does my father want?" I said. "Why does he always have a puck?"

Methuselah, Great Hairless One, Great Wrinkled One, was silent.

6

―――――

N OT LONG before my first confession, my father had taken me aside and told me there was no point in my trying to keep secrets from the priest. A secret was just an unforgiven sin, he said, and besides, while I might fool the priest, I could never fool God, who knew even my most secret thoughts. I had seen the machine room at *The Daily Chronicle*, he said. Well, there was one just like that in heaven, except much bigger. There were thousands, millions of machines in it, just like the ones that automatically typed out the wire-service stories at *The Daily Chronicle*, the stories you saw in the paper with headings like Paris (AP), London (CP). On heaven's teletype, he said, my heading was St. John's (DD). The entire record of my mind was being transcribed by some teletype machine in heaven. As soon as God saw the heading, St. John's (DD), he knew that what followed would be the secret thoughts of Draper Doyle.

For a while, I believed this, and dared not keep even my most embarrassing sins from the priest. I imagined God in some celestial machine room, reading my most secret thoughts the minute I thought them, receiving urgent bulletins from the mind of his St. John's correspondent, Draper Doyle. For all I knew, God was reading my mind aloud on some television newscast in heaven. The CBC. The Celestial Broadcasting Corporation. And now, the CBC news. With God. This just in: A reading from the mind of Draper Doyle. Or my secret thoughts were appearing on the front page of heaven's equivalent of *The*

Daily Chronicle. Imagine the readership. Imagine what an ad would cost.

As time went on, I had become more tickled by this notion than frightened by it, a fact my father somehow sensed, for he soon abandoned it in favour of another. I had been born, he said, with the black mark of original sin on my soul, which was otherwise pure white. It was the kind of black mark the puck leaves on the boards. Each time I sinned, another black mark was made. What I had to watch out for, he said, was that my soul did not go black before my time on earth ran out. For if it did, if it became what he called "puck black," so black that no amount of time in the fires of purgatory could cleanse it, I would have to go to hell. The only thing that would keep my soul from going black before my time on earth ran out was confession. If, throughout my life, I made honest confessions, my soul would go to purgatory, he said, from which, when the cleansing process was complete, it would rise to heaven, with the souls of all those people whose sins had been forgiven. I imagined a host of white pucks, floating up like ash from purgatory.

Even this notion, however, had not been enough to keep me forever honest in confession. In fact, by the time my father died, I was well-advanced in the art of insincere confession. I had found that the best way to avoid blurting out the details of some real and possibly mortal sin was to compile, before going to confession, a list of imaginary sins, the rule of thumb for which was "venial and vague." My list always looked something like this.

Disobeyed mother	3 times
Fought with sister	5 times
Did not pay attention in school	4 times
Forgot to use handkerchief	2 times

My "sinventory," Uncle Reginald called it, when I showed it to him one day. It included only those kinds of venial sins that I knew grownups could imagine me committing—violations, in other words, of what Uncle Reginald called "the junior ten commandments," most of which had to do with hygiene and obedience.

By the time Aunt Phil and Sister Louise intervened that November, I could compile a convincing sinventory in a matter of minutes. It turned out that displaying my stained underwear on the bulletin board in the kitchen was not revenge enough for Aunt Phil—perhaps she thought the real culprits, Mary and my mother, had gotten off scot-free. Though it was quite clearly Aunt Phil's idea, it was Sister Louise who suggested that from now on my mother, Mary, and I go to Father Seymour for confession. Sister Louise and Aunt Phil were already doing so, but the rest of us had been going to the parish priest. Going to Father Seymour, Sister Louise said, might help us get over our father's death more quickly—she was only sorry she hadn't thought of it before.

"It's been seven months now," Sister Louise said, "and, if anything, the three of you seem worse than ever." She looked pointedly at me when she said "the three of you," then gave my mother a conspiratorial wink, as if to say that it was really only me that needed help, but that it might be hard to convince me to go to Father Seymour unless she and Mary did so, too. Once again, I looked to my mother to put a quick stop to what was clearly a bad idea. She seemed about to speak when Aunt Phil broke in.

"I think it's a wonderful idea, Sister," Aunt Phil said, as if, because we were living in her house, the final decision was more hers than ours. She got up and, before anyone realized what she was doing, phoned Father Seymour. "Would it be all right if Linda and the children went to you for confession from now on?" she said, as if this was some special favour that our mother had been too shy to ask of him herself.

Aunt Phil soon after announced that, from now on, we would all go together to confession, the way another family might have gone for haircuts. We went once a week, on Wednesday, which became known as "Confession Wednesday."

"If sin was hair," said Uncle Reginald, who went to neither mass nor confession, "you'd all be bald."

If sin was hair, Sister Louise said, Uncle Reginald would look like Rip van Winkle, with hair down to his ankles, using his beard as a scarf to keep him warm in the wintertime.

Why did it have to be our uncle who heard our confession? I asked Aunt Phil. Surely there was a rule against this sort of thing, people pouring out their sins to relatives, priests hearing the confessions of relatives with whom they would soon have dinner. Mightn't a priest, in such circumstances, show favouritism, assigning less penance than was called for, doling out extra forgiveness to his inlaws? It might have been only this that worried me, to hear me talk, the possibility that we might have an unfair advantage over other people. At any rate, none of my arguments could sway her. We were lucky, she said, to have our own uncle to confess to—look at all the children who had to confess to total strangers. "Lucky them," I said, at which she flicked my earlobe quite painfully with her finger.

I was so distressed at the thought of going to Father Seymour, having to withhold from him such things as Momary dreams and buying my own underwear, that Uncle Reginald devoted a whole session of oralysis to confession. Why did I have to go to confession at all? he said. Why couldn't I just mail my sinventory to Father Seymour and have him mail me my penance? That way, instead of having confession once a week, we could have it once a year. There could be a special form you had to fill out, just like the income tax form. "Sin-come tax" we could call it, he said.

Father Seymour, of course, would require signed receipts from all those people who had suffered at my hands. Uncle Reginald imagined me beating someone up, then asking for a receipt. "Received from Draper Doyle. One punch in the head," signed, "Young Leonard. November 17, 1966." I could send all my sins to Father Seymour once a year, to be audited by him. Then I would keep checking the mailbox for his reply, which would go something like this: "Please say this amount of penance—two thousand Hail Mary's. (Please note the self-defence exemption clause. See Form 2A.)"

Despite oralysis, however, despite all my complaints, we went to Father Seymour. Every Wednesday, after Aunt Phil and our mother came home from work, before we had even sat down to dinner, we went to confession, all of us plodding guiltily to church where Father Seymour was waiting for us, all of us walking with heads bowed—and no wonder, said Uncle Reginald, with a whole week's worth of sins on our shoulders, he was surprised we even made it to confession. Wasn't it possible, I said, that we were overdoing it a little bit?—you couldn't get balder than bald after all.

Aunt Phil assured me that you could never go to confession too often. Did I know, she asked me, that before I had even finished saying penance, sin was re-accumulating on my soul? Uncle Reginald was right, she said, in saying that sin was like hair. Even as the barber was cutting it, she said, your hair was growing, and even as the priest was forgiving you, even as you were saying your penance, sin was re-accumulating on your soul.

While Aunt Phil and our mother took Sister Louise to the sacristy where Father Seymour would hear her confession before he heard ours, Mary and I would kneel side by side in the pew. "Mary," I'd whisper, "we shouldn't have to go to him," and Mary, as if she was fighting the urge to agree with me, to rebel against something her elders had deemed to be right, would make a face and put her hands over her ears. How well I remember them, our mother and Aunt Phil, coming out from the sacristy to take turns genuflecting, then kneeling together in the pew outside the confessional, waiting their turn with the rest of us. When Father Seymour had heard Sister Louise, he would come out across the altar, his confession stole about his shoulders, and hurry down one of the side aisles, taking great care not to look into the pews, acting as if he didn't know that it was Wednesday, that among those penitents who were waiting for him was his entire family with whom he would have dinner afterwards.

Aunt Phil always went in first, then our mother, then Mary, then me. I remember my mother waiting with head bowed for Aunt Phil to finish, getting up to take the door which Aunt Phil held open for her. And I remember best of all that awkward moment when they met, the exchange of the door, Aunt Phil holding it until my mother had ducked beneath her arm, then releasing it and walking away as my mother closed the door behind her, closed it as silently as it was possible to close it, as if she wanted neither Aunt Phil nor Father Seymour to hear her, pulling the door shut by slow degrees and thereby drawing more attention to herself than if she had slammed it with all her might. It would go on for some time, that excruciating fidget with the door, after which, with the final click, the church was once again silent.

Minutes later, my mother would emerge to join Aunt Phil at the altar rail, where once again the two of them would kneel side by side, doing the penance which Father Seymour had assigned them, waiting each other out, it seemed, as if Aunt Phil, despite having several minutes' head start on her penance, didn't want to seem less devout by leaving first, and my mother did not want to make Aunt Phil's penance seem shamefully long by finishing ahead of her.

Despite Vatican II, Aunt Phil kept her head covered in church, and my mother, at her insistence, did the same. And though it was ten years since her husband's death, Aunt Phil still dressed in black when she went out. My mother did, too, though it was understood that, come the first anniversary of my father's death, she would stop doing so. Aunt Phil begrudgingly allowed that it was "acceptable" for a widow to stop wearing black after a year, but her tone implied that a woman of real resolve and devotion would wear black forever. There they were, the two of them, each week, kneeling at the altar rail, wearing their bandannas, dressed so much alike that they might have belonged to the same order, or formed their own, an order of two, the Order of Philomena Clark and Linda Ryan. They would kneel there, far longer than it took anyone to say their penance until, finally, by some sort of signal of body language imperceptible to other people, they would get up at exactly the same time, genuflect together, then go back to the pew and wait for us to finish. Every Wednesday afternoon, this silent set of actions was repeated, exactly, ritually, as if it was part of the sacrament itself.

As for me, I dreaded what Uncle Reginald called my "two minutes in the box" with Father Seymour. I hated the waiting. I remember the murmuring voices from inside the box, the church dark except for a trace of late-afternoon November light coming through the stained glass windows, people going gloomily about. I didn't always go in right after Mary—the rule was that any adults who were waiting went in ahead of children. But Father Seymour always recognized my voice— I could tell my the tone of *his* voice, in which there was a warning against my being in any way familiar with him. The worst part of it for me, aside from the sheer embarrassment of confessing to a relative, was that I was now forced to confess some real sins, for I had to include in my sinventory those sins he had seen me committing, or those he was likely to have heard about from someone else, be it one of the boys of Father Seymour's Number, or Aunt Phil, or even Sister Louise. "Anything else?" he kept saying, "anything else?" whenever I paused on the sinventory, as if there was some particular sin he was waiting for, as if he had his own list on which there were still some sins I had yet to confess, still some not crossed off.

In this manner, he teased from me a confession of wetting the bed those first two times. It hardly seemed possible that this was the "sin" he was waiting for, since even by the loosest definition of the word it wasn't one, but when I mentioned it he seemed satisfied, and then gave me my penance. Every week it went like this. "Anything else?" he'd say, and I'd rack my memory in search of what other sins he might possibly have heard of me committing.

Even worse than confession was the meal that followed it, to which Father Seymour was always invited; his reward, it seemed, for forgiving us our sins. It was clear from the way he carried on that Aunt Phil had not told him about the underwear episode. No man, no priest especially, in the company of a woman who had worn his underwear on her head, would have been as cheerful as Father Seymour. He acted as if we should all have hearty appetites and be in an especially good mood because we had just been to confession. As far as I could see, the only one in an especially good mood was him, which was understandable, for I would have paid any amount of money for the chance to sit around, having dinner with people who had just poured out their sins to me. I'd have been certain to get the upper hand in conversation. Father Seymour made such a show of not taking advantage of the situation that he made matters worse, his joviality only serving to remind us of what he knew, what he had on all of us, so to speak. We might all have been stark naked except for him.

Each week, I stared at my mother, wondering what she had told Father Seymour. Did she worry, too, about what Aunt Phil might or might not have told him? Did she confess things because she believed he already knew about them? Did she worry that if she told him something, he would tell Aunt Phil? Surely not, it seemed to me. Surely, between grownups it was different, altogether different. I stared at Mary, too, for she always seemed especially mortified. I tried to figure out which trap had claimed her this time. Had she foolhardily confessed to some embarrassing sin and was now regretting it, or had she given so glowing an account of herself that Father Seymour had guessed that she was lying?

I never felt more guilt-ridden than I did when leaving the confessional, what with all the lies I told while I was in there.

"Nothing whets the appetite like a clear conscience," said Father Seymour. "Yes," I felt like saying, "and nothing dulls it like liver and onions," which was the standard menu on Confession Wednesdays. It must be true that virtue is its own reward, for every confession day Aunt Phil served liver and onions, with either bread pudding or what Uncle Reginald called "the spookie cookies" for dessert. After the last day of a wake, Aunt Phil would bring home whatever snacks had been left behind in the kitchen at Reg Ryan's. (Though the kitchen was provided by us, the snacks were provided by the mourners.) "No sense letting good food go to waste," she said. Sometimes there were sandwiches, but mostly it was cookies which, for the next several days, would constitute our dessert. The spookie cookies always filled me with revulsion. I could never quite put down the notion of the dear departed getting up in the middle of the night and going to the kitchen for a snack. It was bad enough eating food that you knew had been pawed over by the living.

How I dreaded those spookie cookies. They bothered me so much that Uncle Reginald devoted a full session of oralysis to Aunt Phil's menu. He told me that I should not be surprised that Aunt Phil took better care of our souls than she did of our bodies, the soul being so much less expensive to maintain. He claimed that Aunt Phil was keeping the "good food" for herself. When I looked dubious, he asked me if I thought it was pure coincidence that Aunt Phil was exactly as many pounds overweight as the rest of us combined were underweight. "The very fat of others on her bones," he said.

One of the worst Confession Wednesdays was Ash Wednesday, which happened to fall on my parents' wedding anniversary. We, or I should say the others, ate dinner with what Aunt Phil called "the mark" still on their foreheads. They were not allowed to wipe it off, but had to wait, Aunt Phil said, until it "faded naturally." "Remember Man that thou art dust and unto dust thou shalt return." What I remembered was Father Seymour's thumb, making the sign of the cross in cold ashes on my forehead. Ashes, Young Leonard had told me, from the Protestant crematorium. Only in death, it seemed, only when reduced to ashes, were Protestants of any use to Catholics. We were walking around with human remains on our foreheads, Young Leonard said, a thought which seemed to please him to no end.

Well, I decided that the others could do as they wanted, but I was not about to wait until some dead Protestant "faded naturally" from my forehead. After confession, just before dinner, I put my head beneath the bathroom tap and washed some poor soul down the drain. Then I got one of those magic markers and dabbed the sign of the cross on my forehead, hoping that this would pass for ashes. I felt even more guilty than usual throughout dinner, waiting for someone to notice that I had magic marker on my forehead. There we sat, just back from confession, all with black smudges on our foreheads, guilt vying with a kind of morbid gloom for the upper hand, the six of us (Uncle Reginald was there, but Sister Louise could not make it) eating our liver and onions, after which Aunt Phil came out of the pantry with an especially mouldy-looking batch of spookie cookies.

"I'm not eating them," I said. "No way. The liver and onions were bad enough. Why do we have to have liver anyway?"

"It's good for you," Aunt Phil said. "There's iron in it."

The iron, said Uncle Reginald, was what made it so hard to chew. And being hard to chew made it good for boxers, for it built up the muscles in their jaws, thereby increasing their ability to absorb punches in the face without losing consciousness.

"Great," I said, "that's all I need. An iron jaw."

"Eat your cookies, Draper Doyle," Aunt Phil said.

"No," I said, "I don't want to."

She then launched into a lecture on Father Francis, who lived, she said, "below the equator," making it sound like he was underground, or below the world's paraline perhaps, where everything was dead or dying. "Not everyone in this world enjoys the advantages that you do, young man," she said. "Look at poor José."

Poor José—that seemed to be his name, for it was never just José—was a boy my age who lived in the village in South America where Father Francis's mission was located. I was sure it was no coincidence that, ever since I had started seeing my father's ghost, Father Francis had been writing to Aunt Phil about poor José, describing the awful conditions in which he lived. Getting up from the table, Aunt Phil went to the sideboard and came back with several of Father Francis's letters. She looked pointedly at me. "Father Francis wrote directly to you, young man," she said, as if this fact alone should shame me into eating all my food.

"My dear Newfie Nephew," Aunt Phil read. "How are you? I am feeling fine." There followed yet another instalment of the miseries of poor José. (The Miseries of Poor José. It sounded like the title of some wretched novel, said Uncle Reginald. *The Miseries of Poor José* by Father Francis.) His life had not changed much since the last letter. Poor José never got enough to eat, had so few clothes that he had to wander around half-naked all the time, had no school to go to, no church to attend, no home to speak of. Poor José, Aunt Phil said, had to use the bathroom outdoors while all sorts of wild animals were watching. I told her that, while all of this might be true—and I stressed might, for I suspected that poor José was a product of Aunt Phil's imagination—none of it was my fault.

"I never said it was your fault," Aunt Phil said. "But imagine if poor José knew about all the food that you were wasting."

"But he doesn't know," I said. "Not unless Father Francis tells him. In which case, it's Father Francis's fault, not mine."

"Young man," Aunt Phil said, but Uncle Reginald came to my rescue.

"What possible difference will it make to poor José," said Uncle Reginald, "if Draper Doyle eats all his food?" He went on to wonder if it would comfort poor José to know that I stuffed myself to bursting night after night. Were bulletins being sent to the poor people of South America by the hour, keeping them up to date about what percentage of their food the children of the Western world were eating? Was there a giant score board, perhaps, by which the starving masses of South America kept track of their favourite eaters in North America? To hear Aunt Phil talk, he said, I had my own following in South America, a kind of fan club that watched my meals the way

people in our own country watched sports events, deriving
some strange, vicarious satisfaction from every morsel I managed to force myself to eat. "What do you think poor José
would be like," said Uncle Reginald, "if he was in Draper
Doyle's shoes?"

"He'd thank God he had shoes," Aunt Phil said.

Aunt Phil had often tried to convince me to answer Father
Francis's letters, telling me that his work was so hard that his
spirits were often very low. About all I knew about Father
Francis was that the rules of his order required that he keep his
hood up all the time, even indoors. I couldn't imagine what it
would be like in the heat of South America to have to keep my
hood up. There were twenty priests at the mission, and all I
could picture, when Aunt Phil mentioned Father Francis, was
twenty grown men with hoods up, having dinner. I was sure
that nothing I could say to a man living in such circumstances
would cheer him up.

"Maybe you'll answer this one," Aunt Phil said, when she
finished reading.

I said nothing.

Aunt Phil put the letter back in the envelope and looked at
Uncle Reginald. "The child's impudence I can understand,"
she said. "But you should—"

Just then, without warning of any kind, my mother put
down her fork and started to cry. As if this was the prearranged
signal that the meal was over, Aunt Phil got up and began to
clear the table. We sat there, Father Seymour, Uncle Reginald,
Mary, and I, trying very hard to look as if it was entirely normal
for someone to burst out crying at the dinner table, or perhaps
as if no one *was* crying at the dinner table. When our mother
leaned her ash-smeared forehead on her hand and continued to
cry, Mary pushed back her chair, stood up, and raised a glass of
water in front of her. It might have been something that,

all throughout the meal, she had been trying to work up the nerve to do, at first waiting for the right moment, then, having allowed all the right moments to pass, waiting for the least inappropriate moment. Finally, at exactly that moment when to stand up and propose a toast would be the worst, most mortifying thing to do, she had jumped to her feet and, all but weeping with embarrassment, blurted out "A toast to Mom on her anniversary."

"No, Mary," our mother said, shaking her head and motioning for Mary to sit down. She began to wipe her eyes and, as if to prove that she had stopped crying, she smiled, but Mary pressed on.

"A toast to Mom," Mary said, looking about in panic for someone to join her. She looked beseechingly at me, as if to say that for me to let her down at this moment would be unfair, even by the standards of the war that we had been waging against each other since I was born.

I looked around the table. Aunt Phil, who seemed not to have noticed that Mary was in mid-toast, went on clearing the table. At last Uncle Reginald stood up and solemnly held out his glass of water, winking at my mother as he did. Then Father Seymour rose, and, smiling indulgently, as if to say that toasting your mother with a glass of water was a lovely gesture, raised his glass, at which my mother reddened and, once again starting to cry, asked Mary to sit down.

Mary looked at me again, at which point I stood up, held up my glass, and said "A toast to Mom."

When I tried to touch my glass to hers, however, she pulled away and, smiling, said "Not yet, Draper Doyle."

Our mother sat there, staring at her plate.

"Mom," Mary said, "I'd just like to say—"

Her voice broke and she paused, concentrating on the glass of water. "I'd just like to say—"

Her voice breaking once again, she stopped. Her bottom lip began to quiver and her eyes welled with tears.

"Mom, I'd just like to say that you're—"

Before she could say another word, Aunt Phil reached out and, quite matter-of-factly, as if Mary was extending it to her, plucked the glass of water from her hand. The tears that Mary had been holding back came flooding forth, and as, with considerable embarrassment, the rest of us sat down, she went running to her room, our mother following soon after.

7

R EG RYAN Sr. had left to my father the editorship of what
Uncle Reginald once described as the world's worst newspaper, *The Daily Chronicle*. It was a morning paper, "a mourning
paper," Uncle Reginald said, a paper in mourning for its own
past greatness.

At one time a major paper in the city, back when newspapers were expected, even required to be biased, it had fallen
on hard times. The problem with *The Daily Chronicle* was that
while other papers in the city had changed with the times,
toning down or disguising their biases, it had stayed the same,
continuing to denounce those who, as its editorials often put
it, were of the "wrong" politics or the "wrong" religion.

Even the layout of the paper had stayed the same. Every
morning, *The Daily Chronicle* appeared with an ad for Reg
Ryan's funeral home in the top left corner of the page, and a
short quote from the bible in the top right corner. The quote
was called "The Word of God," and had been appearing in
the top right corner since the first day the paper had been
published. That's how "The Word of God" had become the
nickname for *The Daily Chronicle*, even among people who
liked the paper. "Is The Word of God out yet?" people would
say at newsstands. "I wonder what's keeping The Word of
God today. It's usually out by now." People would read stories
aloud from the paper, concluding by saying "This is The Word
of God."

Always sensational, *The Daily Chronicle*, by the time my father took over, had been a strange combination of scandal sheet and church bulletin. The only thing that distinguished it from other tabloids, apart from the church news, was the complete absence of sex scandal stories, stories which neither Sister Louise nor the other members of the editorial board, Father Seymour and Father Francis, would tolerate. Side by side with stories about how construction of a new church was proceeding were stories about UFO sightings, aliens from other planets, celebrities returning from the dead. Aunt Phil, who spent much of her spare time reading about such things herself, saw nothing wrong with this—"sugaring the pill," she called it. How strange it must have been for my father, who had studied metaphysical philosophy at Oxford, to edit the *Chronicle*. He had often joked that what the paper lacked in philosophy, it more than made up for in metaphysics.

Every morning, when I got up for breakfast, there was a copy of that day's *Daily Chronicle* on the dining-room table, left there by Aunt Phil who, before going to work, had gone through it page by page, assessing the job the new editor—the third since my father's death—was doing. I always looked at the editorial page, the "sermon" as it was known throughout the city. I had delivered my first sermon when I was six years old. That's what my father called it, "delivering the sermon." Depending on whose turn it was to write it, I would stop by the rectory, or the convent, or the orphanage on my way home from school to pick up that day's editorial, then take it to my father at the newsroom. "Here he is," my father always said, "Draper Doyle, delivering the sermon."

Sister Louise, Father Francis, and Father Seymour, "the board," as my father called them, wrote the editorials, which appeared in the paper unsigned, so that most people were under the impression that my father wrote them, an impression which we were all sworn to do nothing to correct. Usually, an editorial was an endorsement of the church's position on some matter, on birth control perhaps, or abortion, or the celibacy of priests. "There's no harm in people thinking that Donald writes them," Sister Louise said. "We're only putting into plain language what Donald would say in that sophisticated way of his."

This was the accepted notion, that while my father's views were doubtless entirely proper, entirely in line with those of the board, he might express them in such a way as to make them incomprehensible to what Sister Louise called "the average reader of the *Chronicle*." This, Sister Louise said, far from being a criticism of him, was to his credit—it was only because the board lacked his ability with language, only because of what she called their "plodding minds," that they were able to make themselves understood by the common person. It was better that my father apply his talents to the running, rather than to the writing, of the paper, she said, especially since he was the only one of them who knew how to run it.

This was how they all talked about him, as a kind of behind-the-scenes genius, on the one hand an adept in the mysterious process of putting out a paper, on the other the family intellectual who had been sent to Oxford to study scholastic philosophy, acquire the arguments, the proofs of Catholicism, and who now could trot them out, to the discomfiture of non-believers, at a moment's notice. It was commonly believed that not even Father Francis or Father Seymour had his command of metaphysics. He knew that this was how they thought about him. He once said they were all waiting for some sidewalk confrontation, during which he would be called upon to quote at length from Thomas Aquinas. The routing of some Protestant in public, in broad daylight, that was what they wanted.

But he had never said as much to them. Sister Louise had disarmed him by making token deferrals to his authority whenever church matters were being discussed. "Donald will correct me if I'm wrong," she'd say, then go on to voice her opinion, while my father sat there, as if in tacit agreement with every word she said.

He had rarely spoken at family gatherings. His often distant, preoccupied manner had been put down to what Sister Louise called "the fineness of his mind." They spoke as if between arcane technical matters on the one hand and metaphysics on the other, most of what went on in my father's mind was incomprehensible to anyone but him. It was for this reason that they were not especially troubled by his breakdown, which had happened when I was five. In fact, they had seemed almost reassured by it, as if it confirmed, beyond all doubt, their assessment of him. It was the kind of thing that people with minds like my father's were known to do, even expected to do, it seemed.

"The mind that man has," Sister Louise said, shaking her head, as if it was inevitable that, from sheer proximity to that divine spark, his body would burn out from time to time.

That it was his body and not his mind that was the problem was obvious, Sister Louise said, from the high spirits he was showing in the hospital. It was a case of sheer physical exhaustion, that's all it was. The wonder, her tone implied, was that it had taken this long to happen. "I wouldn't be surprised if this was just the first of many breakdowns," Sister Louise said, making "breakdown" sound like some sort of benign growth which, every so often, would be removed. Everyone had nodded, as if this observation somehow clinched the matter. He was five weeks in the hospital, then came home without fanfare of any kind—my father, Sister Louise said, was not the kind of man who liked you to make a fuss over him. He went straight back to work, and soon it was as though that five-week interval had never happened.

I was not surprised that, despite his young age, my father had died of a heart attack. One of the reasons we had been able to keep *The Daily Chronicle* afloat was that our father had been willing to work impossibly long hours for next to no salary, running the newsroom more or less by himself and even overseeing the running of the other departments—paste-up, circulation, even advertising. He worked from three in the afternoon to three in the morning, six twelve-hour shifts a week, his only day off being Saturday, because there was no Sunday edition of the *Chronicle*.

Mind you, a seventy-two hour work week was not unusual among the Ryans. The rest of the family put in just as many hours in the other corners of the empire. "It's hard work that got us where we are," Aunt Phil said. "And it's hard work that will keep us there."

The strange thing was that my father had first taken to working impossibly long hours after his breakdown. He had gone from seeing less of his family than most people would have thought proper to hardly seeing them at all. For the last few years of his life, he had all but lived at the newspaper, leaving the house before noon, coming home at four or five in the morning to have breakfast with our mother, then going to bed just as Mary and I were getting up to go to school. Whole days went by without us seeing him. We always ate breakfast in hushed silence for fear of waking him; most of the time, when we came home to lunch, he had already gone back to work.

Every day, my mother said, the same scene of panic was repeated. Every day, my father was convinced of the absolute impossibility of getting the paper out by six o'clock the next morning, but somehow, every morning without fail, *The Daily Chronicle* appeared. Each morning's issue was a miracle, Aunt Phil said, another routine miracle from Donald Ryan.

During the last few months of his life, we had seen him so infrequently, he had seemed more like a boarder than a husband or a father. "The boarder," in fact, was what our mother had taken to calling him. It was hard to believe, she said, that two people who lived in the same house could see so little of each other. And Mary and I saw him even less than she did. You could count on the fingers of one hand, she said, the number of hours in a week that we were all at home and all awake at the same time. She had begun joking with Mary and me about how the three of us might not be the only ones living in the house, that she was beginning to suspect that someone else, "possibly a man," was living with us. She had seen evidence, she said, that a man might be hiding from us, sneaking out to use the toaster while we were sleeping, running water late at night, leaving doors and windows open. Yes, she was almost certain that some fourth person was in the house, leading a kind of shadow existence, a life parallel to ours but somehow never intersecting with it.

This was only a slight exaggeration. At the end, aside from a few hours here and there, his life had only coincided with ours from noon on Saturday when he got up, to early afternoon on Sunday when he began another week of work. It occurred to me, sitting in Aunt Phil's dining room, eating my breakfast while Reg Ryan Sr. looked down from the wall, that it was the ghost of a ghost that I had been seeing lately, the ghost of the ghost my father had been while he was still alive. These were literally his old haunts that he was returning to, for his existence now was hardly less solitary, less disembodied than it had been before his death. I remembered how my mother had looked in the weeks after he was buried. She had seemed more puzzled than anything else, as if his premature death was just the latest inscrutable thing that he had done. For her, his death might have been no more than a completion of, a perfection of, the absence that had been his life.

Some mornings, I had woken up to the sound of Aunt Phil downstairs in our kitchen. She would come over from next door, barge in unannounced to talk to my father, to give him what amounted to his morning pep talk, despite the fact that his day was just ending. The ink was not dry on that morning's paper, and she was already hounding him about tomorrow's. She always told him that the family was counting on him to keep the paper going, "to keep it alive," as she put it.

The phrase conjures up for me now a vision of my father running around in the machine room in which the wire-service machines spewed out copy, day and night, copy that, because we could not afford reporters, comprised about ninety-nine per cent of the paper. I could see my father loading the teletypes, the life-support systems of *The Daily Chronicle*, frantic about them breaking down or running out of paper when he was not there to reload them—my father, endlessly maintaining those machines, the ceaseless noise of which drowned out all other sounds.

One day, when I had gone to the newsroom to deliver the sermon, I was told that my father was in the machine room. I went to the door of the room and was about to knock when, looking through the window, I saw him, bending over one of the teletype machines. At first, I thought he was reading the printout, but then I saw that the movement of his head was too exaggerated. In addition to moving from left to right, following with a kind of mock fascination each line of type across the page, his head was going rapidly up and down, as if he was mimicking the striking of the keys, or else pretending that he was making them move, that he was typing at this impossible speed by sheer telepathy. He stood there mocking that machine, until he happened to look up to catch me staring at him.

I smiled, thinking I had caught him in some harmless game that he was fond of playing. Without straightening up, still with his hands on either side of the teletype, he stared at me for what

seemed like a very long time, then said something. I couldn't
hear him, anymore than I could hear the machines, for the room,
because it bordered the newsroom, was soundproof. When I
shook my head to indicate I hadn't heard, he spoke again, his
lips moving soundlessly. Again I shook my head, and again he
spoke, his face now expressing irritation with what he seemed
to think was my stubborn refusal to hear what he was saying. I
pointed to indicate that I was coming in, at which his expression switched to rage, and he began shouting, shouting soundlessly at me, still bent over that machine, still looking at me
sideways. I began to wonder if he had somehow failed to recognize me. I stood there a little longer, staring at the soundless
tantrum he was throwing, then turned and, dropping the sermon on the desk, ran from the newsroom. He never afterwards
said one word about it.

✦

I could think of only two things our family had done together
on anything like a regular basis—one was watch the hockey
game on Saturday night, and the other was go to early mass on
Sunday morning. It had been Aunt Phil's practice to, as Uncle
Reginald put it, "convene" a meeting of the Divine Ryans at
her house whenever the Habs were playing the Leafs on TV.
There had been no meetings since my father's death last March,
not even during the playoffs in the spring when the Habs had
won their second straight Stanley Cup. When, at dinner one
night, Aunt Phil announced that the whole family was getting
together for the Habs' first televised game of the season this
coming Saturday, I screamed "hurray," causing Mary and my
mother to roll their eyes.

"You're not normal, Draper Doyle," Mary said. "You're a
fanatic."

"What's a fanatic?" I said.

"A fanatic," said Uncle Reginald, "is a fan who is so crazy you have to keep him in the attic."

"It's only a hockey game you know, Draper Doyle," Mary said.

"The Habs have won more Cups than any other team," I said. "Thirteen."

"Why do you like statistics so much, Draper Doyle?" Mary said. "They're only numbers, you know." Mary had a habit of reducing things to their basic elements to prove their worthlessness. "Why do you like all that candy?" she'd say. "Candy's only sugar, you know." Anything that could thus be broken down was worthless, as far as she was concerned.

"Hockey," she said, "all it is is people hitting a piece of rubber back and forth with sticks."

"Water," I said, "all it is is hydrogen and oxygen. Why drink it?"

"Just tell me one thing, Draper Doyle," Mary said. "Do you hate the other teams?"

"Yes," I said.

"They're human beings too, you know," she said.

"No, they're not," I said.

"Look," she said, "I'm not saying Montreal is not the best team. I know they are." The inevitable superiority of the Montreal Canadiens was something to which Mary was resigned, a concession she begrudgingly allowed me whenever we had these arguments, which was often. "I just want you to admit," she said, "that the Boston Bruins for instance are human beings too."

"They're not," I said. "Canadiens are human beings. But Bruins are bears. Black Hawks are birds. Red Wings are birds. Leafs are plants."

"What about the Rangers, Draper Doyle?" my mother said, looking triumphantly around the table. "Aren't they human?

Aren't they?" I had forgotten about those damned Rangers. What were Rangers anyway—forest rangers? Were they human beings? I supposed they were. The New York Rangers hadn't won the Stanley Cup since 1947, but they were human beings, any way you looked at it. I thought about pointing out that Smokey the Bear was a Ranger, but decided against it.

"Shot down, Draper Doyle," Mary said, "shot down." Getting up from the table, she stretched out her arms and made the noise of an airplane, then did a sudden nosedive to the floor. "Boom," she said, so loudly that Aunt Phil was startled. "Shot down," she said, sitting down again.

"You never shot me down," I said. "Mom did."

My defeat at the dinner table notwithstanding, I could hardly sit still for excitement when Saturday arrived. Another season had begun. All week, I had been able to think of nothing else. The Habs had won the Cup the last two years, and had won their first five road games of the season. They seemed unbeatable. Now they were coming home to the Forum. I brought out my many hockey souvenirs from the closet, including a puck which my father had given me when I was seven. It had previously occurred to me that some sort of connection might exist between this puck and the one my father had lately been appearing with, though I couldn't imagine what that connection might be. On a piece of paper taped to one side of the puck, these words were written: "Deflected into the stands by Canadiens goalie Gerry MacNeil at 1:03 of overtime. Caught by Donald Ryan. Nineteen seconds later, Elmer Lach scored to win the Stanley Cup for Montreal. Montreal Forum, April 16, 1953." How I envied my father. I'd have given anything to be there when the Habs won the Cup.

Among my other hockey souvenirs, the most unlikely of the lot was a hardbound copy of the *Aeneid* which my father had given me for my birthday when I was five, an illustrated adaptation for children. *The Cartoon Virgil*, it was called. The full-page drawings were in the manner of the old *Classics Illustrated* comic books, full of lurid detail—I can still see the Frightful Forms, Death-dealing War, and Mad Discord with "snaky, bloodstained hair." I knew *The Cartoon Virgil* by heart. Of all the adapted classics my father had had me read, I liked it best, particularly those parts which took place in the underworld. (There were also underworlds in *The Cartoon Homer* and *The Cartoon Dante*, but Virgil's was my favourite.) My father had shown me how the black, laminated cloth cover of *The Cartoon Virgil* could itself be a kind of underworld. On Saturday nights, I always had to go to bed after the first period of the hockey game, so my father, using a pen that had run out of ink, would "write" the score of the game on the cover of *The Cartoon Virgil*. At breakfast, after mass on Sunday mornings. I would put a sheet of paper over the book and shade it with a pencil until I found the score. "Here it comes," my father would say, "here it comes, emerging from the underworld."

And so it would. A kind of ghost of what he had written would appear. Montreal 5 – New York 3. After a while, there were so many scores invisibly engraved in the cover of the book that my father had to start writing in the date to help me tell them apart. Montreal 3 – Toronto 3, 02/12/65. A kind of memory slate is what the book became, for, in the process of trying to find the score of last night's game, I would call up the scores of games played years ago, and we would stop at each one to see if we remembered it. Scattered haphazardly across the cover of *The Cartoon Virgil* in my father's handwriting were the scores of every televised Habs game from 1963 to 1966 when, because I was then allowed to stay up late, my father had stopped writing them. From then on, I had written the scores on the cover myself, with the used-out pen my father had given me.

Now, to remind me to write the score and date of tonight's game on the book, I laid the pen on the cover of *The Cartoon Virgil* and went downstairs just as Uncle Reginald was descending in the lift. We were both wearing Habs sweaters, his with number 9 and mine with number 4 on the back. "Good evening hockey fans from ghost to ghost," said Uncle Reginald. I grinned.

Aunt Phil, Sister Louise, and Father Seymour were already in the living room when we got there. None of them had any real affection for hockey. As far as they were concerned, God had created hockey for the sole purpose of allowing Catholics to humiliate Protestants on nationwide TV. Most of Fleming Street was Catholic, but there were a few Protestant families. In fact, one of the city's staunchest Protestants and monarchists lived near the end of the street, her house just visible from Aunt Phil's. Millie Barter was in every way Aunt Phil's opposite—a tiny, fragile woman who, according to Aunt Phil, considered work to be beneath not only her, but her entire family. The Barters were supposed to be distantly related to some obscure, umpteen-times-removed cousin of the Queen, prompting Aunt Phil to refer to Millie as Queen Millie and to her family as The Royal Family. The Barters had a fortune, said to be so old that even they could not remember how they came by it. The Barters, Aunt Phil said, had done nothing since coming to the New World but live off some Old World fortune. God only knew where their money came from, she said. They had lived on that side of the street for as long as the Ryans had lived on this side, and in all that time, no Barter had ever been seen to do a day's work. As far as Aunt Phil was concerned, all Millie Barter did was back such Protestant causes as the retention of the Union Jack and royal visits.

Despite the fact that the Ryans and the Barters had never spoken to each other, it had somehow become the custom that

after each televised game between the Habs and the Leafs, the
family whose team had won would phone the family whose
team had lost, not to speak to them, of course, but only to let
their phone ring three times—three rings, three gloating cheers.
Just as the Americans and the Russians had the hotline, the
Ryans and the Barters had what Uncle Reginald called "the
knellephone," their only cold war communication.

Aunt Phil stood at her bedroom window just before the
game, peeking out through the curtains, watching the Barter
children arrive at what she derisively called Buckingham Palace.
"Here they come," she said, "The Royal Family." Aunt Phil
followed the comings and goings of the Barters as closely as
other people did the real royal family. She began to announce
their arrivals like some palace doorman. "Prince Pimple-puss,"
she said scornfully, "accompanied by his wife, Princess Pasty-
face, and Child William, the Earl of Dirty Diapers." Laughing,
Uncle Reginald wondered if Millie Barter referred to Aunt
Phil's house as the Vatican, and watched it as closely as Aunt
Phil watched hers. Perhaps she too had nicknames for all of us,
he said.

"Like what?" I said.

"Well," he said, "what about His Mouldiness, Reg Ryan?
What about The Infallible Philomena?"

"Don't be absurd," Aunt Phil shouted from her bedroom.
"Don't be putting ideas in the boy's head."

Then she came out and, as she always did before a Habs/
Leafs game, put the phone on top of the television set.

"We'll ring that woman's phone tonight, Draper Doyle,"
she said, "you just watch."

"Maybe she'll ring ours, Aunt Phil," Mary said, exchanging
a smile with my mother.

When Montreal was playing Toronto at the Forum, as they
were tonight, it was not a hockey game, but a holy war, a crusade

carried on nationwide TV, Rome's Canadiens versus Canterbury's Maple Leafs, "the Heathen Leafs against the Holy Habs," as Uncle Reginald put it. Uncle Reginald said that the real coach of the Montreal Canadiens was the pope, who was sending Toe Blake instructions from the Vatican, where he and his cardinals were watching the game on closed-circuit television.

As it turned out, the pope and his cardinals had seen better days, because to everyone's astonishment the Leafs took a 3 − 1 lead in the first period. Never mind the Leafs, Uncle Reginald said, assuring us that, between periods, the pope and his cardinals would find a way of beating them. No one, he said, no one on the face of the earth knew more about hockey than Pope Paul VI. And no one knew less about it than Aunt Phil, I felt like saying. All Aunt Phil knew or wanted to know about the Leafs was that they were Protestant. Throughout the first period, because she was never entirely sure when something helpful to the Habs' cause was happening, she had me sit beside her and, in a low, confidential voice, asked me questions from time to time. When, near the end of the period, Montreal scored to make it 3 − 2 and the room erupted, she waited for the noise to die down, then said the score of the game as if she was keeping track for those who didn't know hockey as well as she did. "Three-two Toronto," Aunt Phil said.

It was a strange sight indeed, a roomful of people who otherwise never watched a hockey game, including Sister Louise and Father Seymour in their habits, acting as if their lives depended on the outcome. "C'mon Montreal," Sister Louise said, leaning forward in her chair, rocking back and forth. Father Seymour, standing up with arms tightly folded, would advance towards the television each time the Habs went up the ice, backing away when they failed to score.

The trouble was, Father Seymour knew almost as little about hockey as Aunt Phil and Sister Louise. "Yes," he said, when the puck bounced off Henri Richard's backside and somehow found its way into the net; "Yes," nodding his head, as if he had seen the goal shaping up, as if it was a classic example of the skill for which the Montreal Canadiens were famous. "It was a fluke," I said scornfully, looking at Uncle Reginald who winked at me and shook his head slightly. It seemed to me that, as well as being a warning, the wink was also meant to tell me that he, too, was thinking of my father.

I remembered the way my father had acted the last few times we had gathered for a game. For someone who knew so much about hockey, he had been very subdued while watching it. He had sat there, in the corner armchair, staring at the television set, speaking only when someone spoke to him, smiling when the Habs scored, or rather when, by the cheer that went up, it was evident that the Habs had scored, for he hadn't seemed to notice until then.

Halfway through the second period, with the Habs down 4 – 3 but coming back, Aunt Phil started in with her very annoying habit of calling the Leafs "the Leaves."

"It's not the Leaves," I said. "It's the Leafs."

"The plural of leaf is leaves, is it not?" Aunt Phil said.

"Yes," I said, "but no one calls them that. They're called the Leafs."

"Why?"

"I don't know why, they just are."

"Well that's not good enough for me. I'll call them the Leaves until someone shows me why I shouldn't call them that."

"Didn't I just show you?" I said. I could just see her correcting this "mistake" in the next edition of *The Daily Chronicle*, the Leafs turning up as the Leaves all over the sports page.

Then Father Seymour joined in, joking about Protestants giving their team a name that contained a mistake in spelling, thereby leaving millions of people with no choice but to make the same mistake, over and over. "Well, I won't make it," Aunt Phil said.

"They score," screamed Danny Gallivan, and he didn't mean the Habs. I felt like telling Aunt Phil that it was her fault. I knew that because I had taken her up on it, she would say "Leaves" as often as possible throughout the evening and I knew that this would so irritate me that the Canadiens were bound to lose. I had a theory that any team's fortune depended on the mood of their fans, the spirit in which they viewed the game. I further believed that, on any particular night, this mood, this spirit, was the same among all their fans throughout the country. At this very moment, all across the country, I believed, Habs fans were becoming irritated, and this did not bode well for their team. It was still possible to turn the mood around, however. All we had to do was concentrate, focus on the game, try to ignore everything else.

At the start of the third period, I set about doing exactly that. I lay down on the floor in front of the television set and had soon regained my concentration to the point where the Habs scored to make it 5 – 4 when Father Seymour sat down on the floor beside me. I knew what was coming. It was his make-contact-with-the-boy routine. I could imagine how Aunt Phil and Sister Louise were smiling at each other, no doubt charmed by the sight of Father Seymour doing what they thought he did best. "Hello Draper Doyle," he said, sitting cross-legged beside me. He picked up my Pepsi and took a sip from it, and as if by this, some sort of bond had been established between us, laid his arm lightly on my shoulder.

"Do you know what the CH on Montreal's uniform stands for, Draper Doyle?" Father Seymour said.

"Yes," I said, "Canadiens/Habitants." Father Seymour said nothing, only looked around the room as if to see if anyone had heard us. Then he informed me that CH were the letters with which the words "church" began and ended. I nodded and went back to watching the game. I tried to think of a way to hurry his routine to its inevitable conclusion before the Leafs scored again.

"But you know," he said, "the word means nothing unless 'u r' in it." I must have looked mystified, for he laughed. "Do you get it, Draper Doyle?" he said, looking around the room. "U r in church. The word 'church' means nothing unless u r in it."

I rolled my eyes and, once again, rather nervously this time, Father Seymour looked around the room. I considered pointing out that UR stood for Uncle Reginald who hadn't been inside a church in twenty years, but thought better of it. Then he got up and went back to standing between Aunt Phil and Uncle Reginald, his arms folded, eyes intently focussed on the television set.

Once again, I set about concentrating on the game. By now, however, my mood was all wrong. There was no way the Canadiens would win with me feeling so anxious and irritated. "They score," screamed Danny Gallivan, and once again he didn't mean the Habs. The Leafs had put one into the empty net to make it 6 − 4, which was how it ended. When the siren sounded, to end the game I saw that Father Seymour was looking at me as if he was about to say something. The Leafs had won, Uncle Reginald said, despite Richard's fluky goal and despite the infallibility of our team's coach. It was obvious that Mary and my mother were delighted to have witnessed one of Montreal's rare defeats, though they didn't dare show it openly, what with everyone else looking the way they normally did at wakes. Mary gave me one of her "inside I'm celebrating" looks and my mother kept her head down to hide a smile that was pulling at the corners of her mouth.

"Toronto 6 – Montreal 4," Mary said.

"That's nothing," said Father Seymour. "It's only one game."

"But it was the first game," I shouted at him, on the verge of tears. "The first game!" by which I meant not only the first of the season, but the first since my father had died, a fact which, though it had gone unmentioned, had obviously been on everyone's mind.

"Don't you speak to me like that, young man," said Father Seymour, advancing towards me, then looking at my mother in a kind of "I really think that was uncalled for" sort of way.

"Draper Doyle didn't mean anything by that, Father," my mother said, her voice strained with embarrassment. "He's just tired, that's all. Apologize to Father Seymour, Draper Doyle."

"I'm sorry," I said, feeling my face flush as Father Seymour, rising on his toes, looked down at me. My apology seemed to settle things. "The Habs will win the next one, Draper Doyle," he said. I nodded and gave him the smile I knew everyone was waiting for.

The prevailing opinion was that the game was a minor set-back, the kind of defeat that would make victory that much sweeter when it came. Of course, there was still one thing left to do. We had to wait for the knellephone to ring, for Millie Barter to break the cold war silence for as long as it took the phone to ring three times. It had been ten minutes since the game ended, and the phone on top of the television set had yet to ring.

"She's making us wait," Aunt Phil said. "She always does."

We sat there for another ten minutes, in silence now that the TV had been turned off. We sat there, looking at that mournfully black phone until it rang at last, the first ring causing all of us to jump, then the second ring, then finally the third which trailed off into a kind of shrill silence.

"Ask not for whom the phone rings," said Uncle Reginald. "It rings for us."

Because I had always gone to bed right after the game and the next morning had gone to mass before breakfast, the hockey game and the mass, separated only by an interval of dreamless, timeless sleep, had seemed to run together. The Sunday after the Habs lost their home opener was no different. Weary from having stayed up late, I only half heard what the priest was saying, and the fact that the priest was Father Seymour, whose voice I had also heard throughout the game the night before, further added to my confusion. As I stood there in the pew, still half asleep, the dreams I had been too tired to have the night before began, snatches of Father Seymour's mass mixing with the play-by-play of both Danny Gallivan and Foster Hewitt, so that a kind of hockey liturgy went running through my mind, a strange game in which there were swirling litanies of saints and hockey players, and the Habs and the Leafs were being asked to pray for one another, a game in which St. Peter was "ad libbing his way to centre ice" and Toe Blake was saying "Upon this Rocket, I will build my Church."

I saw the referee and two opposing centremen line up for the face-off. But instead of dropping the puck, the referee broke it in half, held the pieces above his head for a moment, then gave one piece to each player. "Do this in memory of me," he said. Then, at the sound of the angelus bells, I thought our phone was ringing, ringing three times for someone or something that was lost. I turned and, looking out through the halo of one of the saints in the stained-glass window beside the pew, I saw my father, walking slowly up Fleming Street, his hands in his pockets, as if he was headed to work, headed to *The Daily Chronicle* perhaps, despite the fact that it was Sunday morning.

Through the yellow-tinted glass of the halo of St. Anthony I saw him stop suddenly and turn towards the church, then raise one arm as if to wave to me. Then I saw that there was a puck in his hand. He held it to one side of his head, between thumb and forefinger. He might have been a hockey player, posing with the puck he had used to reach some milestone in his career. But he kept glancing back and forth from me to the puck, a look of quizzical distress on his face.

I decided to wave to him, to tell him to come inside with the rest of us. I removed my hand from the pew in front of me, the hand which, as it turned out, was all that was keeping me up, for I had been asleep on my feet and now woke to find that I had fallen forward against the pews, and then to the floor. I sprawled out on the kneeler, my legs on either side of it, wrapping my arms around it and resting my head against the soft cushion. I would quite certainly have gone to sleep had my mother not reached down and, without so much as taking her eyes off her prayer book, grabbed hold of my blazer collar and pulled me to my feet.

Mary, in a vain attempt to hide this spectacle from the people in the pew behind us, not to mention Aunt Phil who was standing beside her, began taking off her coat, shielding me with it. "Draper Doyle," she whispered, a threat through clenched teeth; then had me stand between her and the pew, pressing me against it, so that while I might still fall asleep, it was quite impossible for me to fall down.

I looked again through the halo to find that, now, Fleming Street was empty. It might have been some old photograph that I was looking at, some yellowed picture of Fleming Street that had appeared in *The Daily Chronicle* a hundred years ago. With the soft and surprisingly pleasant warmth of Mary's body pressed against me, I once again began to dream.

8

———

THE WEEKS leading up to Christmas seemed to be an endless succession of corny movies, most of them, as luck would have it, featuring priests and nuns and orphans. We were forced to sit through *Boys' Town*, *Going My Way*, and *The Bells of St. Mary's*, all of which moved Aunt Phil to tears and even made Sister Louise and Father Seymour look a little wistful. Uncle Reginald observed that Father Seymour was a cross between Spencer Tracy and Bing Crosby, which pleased Aunt Phil until he pointed out that what he meant was that Father Seymour sang like Spencer Tracy and acted like Bing Crosby.

We spent half our time lampooning Aunt Phil's favourites. "He ain't heavy, Fadder, he's my brudder," Mary kept saying, as, with eyes bulging and face beet red, she strained to lift me from the chesterfield. The day after we watched yet another version of *A Christmas Carol*, Uncle Reginald devoted a full session of oralysis to it. He invented something called the Tiny Timometer, an instrument which measured cuteness, and said that we should take readings from it throughout Christmas, especially when corny movies were playing. Every night after that, as we sat watching the likes of Hayley Mills and Julie Andrews succumbing to the call of the convent while angels sang and light came breaking through the clouds, Uncle Reginald would consult the Tiny Timometer, take readings and announce them to the living room.

The lowest reading on the Tiny Timometer, "the least nauseating," as Uncle Reginald put it, was "God bless us, everyone," which he would have me say in the most puny, pathetic voice whenever some corny movie was about to start. Next nauseating on the Tiny Timometer, warranted by any scene in which Bing Crosby broke into song, was "Oh Mother, will there be no plum pudding this year?" The highest reading, that of supremely nauseating came from the mouth of, as Uncle Reginald called him, "That Bobsequious Cratchett," who, shortly after being fired by Ebenezer Scrooge, said "He's not such a bad man, Mother." "He's not such a bad man, Mother," Uncle Reginald would say, whenever our heroes forgave their enemies some heinous crime.

I often played Tiny Tim to Uncle Reginald's Scrooge, or Uncle Scrooginald, as he called himself. "Please Mr. Scrooge," I'd say, "something to eat for my little sister."

"I will give you," Uncle Scrooginald would say, "in exchange for your wheelchair and your sister's crutch, and all the clothes that you and your sister have on your backs, one cup of lukewarm water."

"Oh God bless you, Mr. Scrooge," I'd say, "God bless you, you're a saint."

Other times, I played Scrooge's nephew, blurting out "I say, Uncle, make merry," whenever Uncle Reginald was looking glum. Uncle Reginald would respond, "I say, nephew, if you persist in this nauseating cheerfulness, I shall make pudding of your plums."

The relevance of *A Christmas Carol* to the visitations I was having was not lost on Uncle Reginald. Perhaps, he said, I should do like Scrooge, and the next time my father appeared, dismiss him as a bit of undigested beef.

"You wouldn't think," Aunt Phil said, "that a man would make jokes about a brother not six months in the grave."

In the days leading up to Christmas Day, Mary kept giving me looks that told me that her annual solemn declaration of love was in the offing. Every year, Mary for some reason felt the need and somehow worked up the nerve to say she loved me. This year, she did it in a Christmas card. "Merry Christmas, Draper Doyle," the card said, "I love you," the word love underlined three times.

Nor was this year any different for what happened afterwards. As always, Mary regretted telling me she loved me the minute she did it. "Oh my God," she said, "I can't believe I said 'I love you,' on that card." Mortified to the point of speechlessness by the card, I now had to reassure her that it had seemed entirely appropriate. "No, no," I said, in a tone that begged her not to pursue the matter any further. "It was nice."

"NICE?" Mary said. "NICE? Nice if we were married maybe. Nice if we had about fifty kids. My God, why do I do these things, why?"

Father Seymour gave my mother a necklace, a gesture seen by most of the adults as being both charming and proper from a priest to a sister-in-law who had recently been widowed, who, for the first time in years, had no husband to give her gifts at Christmas. Aunt Phil seemed to think that the necklace would cinch my mother's membership in Father Seymour's Other Number. As it turned out, it had just the opposite effect. There was an awkward moment, or more like an awkward ten minutes when, on Aunt Phil's insistence, Father Seymour tried to put the necklace around my mother's neck. He was tall enough, but unfortunately tried to put it on from the front and stood for an embarrassing amount of time more or less face to face with my mother's bosom, more or less embracing her, while she tried to smile and he struggled to join the clasp of a necklace for perhaps the first time in his life.

No one wanted to acknowledge the awkwardness of what was happening by telling him to put it on from behind.

There they were, my mother and Father Seymour in the middle of the room, my mother leaning as far forward in her high heels as she dared, her arms limp at her sides, as if she was terrified of somehow, inadvertently, throwing them around him, Father Seymour standing on tiptoe, trying both to get closer to the necklace and further from my mother, his whole body showing the strain of this impossibility. How precariously balanced each of them was. It looked as if, at any moment, one of them might topple forwards, straight into the arms of the other, as if this great show they were making of not touching one another would end with them falling to the floor in a kind of mad, we'll-both-be-damned embrace right in the middle of Aunt Phil's living room.

So we all sat there watching them, Sister Louise and Aunt Phil trying hard to seem charmed by their predicament, smiling at them. Aunt Phil kept glancing towards the front door as if she was worried that someone who might misunderstand the situation would suddenly barge in. It seemed it would never end, this strange embrace. There were shouts of what was meant to sound like mock encouragement, as if we were all so relaxed with what was happening that we really didn't care how long it took. "Come on, Father," said Aunt Phil, using her best not-in-the-least-distressed tone of voice. "You can tell he hasn't had much experience," Sister Louise said, which brought a great roar of laughter that trailed off badly and made everyone feel even worse. Finally, his face bursting red, Father Seymour somehow managed it, then raised his arms slowly from our mother's shoulders as if, at the slightest touch, the necklace might come undone. "Ta-dah" someone said, and everyone applauded.

Once each year, at Christmas, after some drinks and much encouragement, Father Seymour agreed to dance, and this year was no different. He took off his jacket, removed his collar and went out into the hall, where the floor was hardwood and where he could be seen from all parts of the living room. I was relieved to see that he did not wear that eager-to-please expression which he coached the boys in his Number to wear. Instead, he stared at his feet most of the time, only now and then looking up with what might have been an expression of humility on his face, as if he was saying either that what he was doing was no big deal, or that he himself could not, perhaps absolutely would not, take any personal credit for it. How seriously they watched him, the grownups, their expressions betraying only the faintest trace of irony.

It was tap-dancing at its best that we were seeing, their faces seemed to say, a master practitioner of an ancient, now declining art. What I felt, more than anything, was sheer astonishment. It was somehow off-putting to know that the man who forgave your sins was fond of tap-dancing. Here was Father Seymour, his white socks and black shoes a blur as he went through his routine, Father Seymour without his collar, his shirt two buttons open, his chest hair showing.

There was much applause when he was finished, by which time he was sweating quite a bit, mopping his brow with his handkerchief, smiling quite boyishly, as if he was some child who each year was coaxed into dancing for his relatives. For how many years before I came along had he been doing it? I wondered. How old was this command performance?

For a moment, I could see the boy he must have been on that first occasion, grinning sheepishly when praised, looking about the room to see the effect that he was having. Now, it was as though there was a kind of sacrifice in it, a sacrifice on his part, as though, for some reason that none of them could quite have put their fingers on, it was important that once a year he indulge in this display that even to them seemed faintly absurd. How they gathered about him afterwards, shaking his hand, slapping him on the shoulder, again with only the faintest trace of irony in their smiles, as if he had suffered some humiliation on their behalf, as if they were congratulating him, not so much on his performance as on the fact that it was over for another year, on his having endured it, somehow for their sake. The Divine Ryans. Uncle Reginald said they had first been called that almost two hundred years ago.

The Christmas recital came just after Christmas, early in the new year. Father Seymour, still unwilling to own up to my mother and Aunt Phil about his failure, or rather his refusal, to make me part of the chorus, told me that I would appear on stage with the choir, not singing, of course, but pretending to sing, "lip-synching," he said. "Just move your mouth like you're singing the words," he said. When I looked doubtful, he put his hands on my shoulders. "Now, you'll do it, Draper Doyle," he said. "And it will be our secret, won't it? You don't want to disappoint your mother, do you?" I shook my head.

In the days leading up to the recital, my mother kept asking me to sing my part.

"C'mon, Draper Doyle," she said. "Let's hear it."

"I'm in the chorus," I said, trying to sound casually dismissive, "I can't sing by myself."

I was at least relieved that I would not be among the dancers, there being no known way to fake tap-dancing—tap-synching, perhaps? Moving to the sound of someone else's feet?

The day before the concert, Aunt Phil took me to Parker's barbershop where, for some reason, there were pictures on the wall of boys my age with various hairstyles. I say "for some reason" because the only haircut Mr. Parker knew was the brush-cut, which he promptly gave me. ("Men have hair there, too," my mother had said. Imagine if, like the hair on your head, it just kept growing. I could see myself choosing, from pictures on Mr. Parker's wall, what style I wanted.)

I spent most of that night in front of the mirror, begging my hair to grow, pulling on it, one hair at a time. I might have used my mother's eyebrow tweezers except I was worried that instead of making the hairs longer, I might just pull them out altogether, leaving my head completely bald, not to mention covered with red dots. I got my mother's mirror and had a mock consultation with Methuselah.

"Oh Great Hairless One," I said, "oh Great Wrinkled One, oh Oracle of Oracles, oh Prune of Prunes, oh Wisest of the Wise, tell me all."

"What is your question?" said Methuselah.

"Will my mother notice that I'm not singing?" I said. That sage of sages, that centre of the world's wisdom, just sat there, looking back at me.

✦

The only full-length mirror in the house was in the hall, and, while they were getting ready for the recital, Aunt Phil and my mother took turns using it, going back and forth without speaking to each other. Once, they shared it, Aunt Phil standing just behind my mother. For a moment their eyes met in the mirror. My mother seemed surprised, but Aunt Phil, as if she believed she was still looking at herself, stood as my mother was standing and, in perfect imitation of her, touched her throat softly with her fingers. Then, my mother smiled and, as if to conform to what she still thought was her own reflection, Aunt Phil smiled back. Finally, something broke the spell. Aunt Phil, addressing what she now realized was my mother's image in the mirror, said "Don't you smile at me." When my mother, her face protesting her innocence, gestured to the mirror, as if to accuse it of having played a trick on both of them, Aunt Phil turned away.

My mother belonged to a family even older than the Ryans, a once-great family whose fortune was long since spent, and whose members had begun to scatter even before some of them came across from Ireland in the nineteenth century. Her parents had died before I was born and her two sisters, her only close relatives, were living on the mainland. Delaney, my mother's maiden name, was a good name according to Aunt Phil, who spoke not of good and bad families but of good and bad names. All Protestant names were bad, of course, but so were most Catholic names as far as she was concerned. A family had a bad name if it had a bad history or, even worse, no history at all. Delaney was still a good name when our mother joined the family. "No money but good blood" was how Aunt Phil put it, and since the Ryans' own fortune was declining, it must have seemed there were no real grounds for complaint. Besides all this, there was our mother herself, who, within the circle of church families in the city, was thought to have been something of a catch. People had talked about how Donald Ryan was soon to marry "that tall Delaney girl." Do you, Donald Ryan, take that tall Delaney girl to be your wife? was how I had often imagined their wedding.

We walked into St. Martin's Hall together, all the Divine Ryans, made the kind of entrance we knew people were expecting, first Father Seymour pushing Sister Louise, then Aunt Phil leading me by the hand, then my mother walking side by side with Mary, and finally Uncle Reginald, not dressed in his uniform, of course, but looking impressive nonetheless, walking with that mournful grace he had, and looking about as if he really was head of the family, as if the train in front of him was his creation. Everyone turned to look at us, and a wave of whispering went down the hall. How many of them, I wondered, could have imagined my mother and Aunt Phil working at Reg Ryan's, vacuuming beneath the caskets, polishing the brass and silver handles?

For there was Aunt Phil, the famous Philomena, and there was our mother, a fixture at her side, "the Young Widow," as she was called: "the Young Widow," people whispered, as if this was her official title, bestowed upon her by the Ryans, as if she was the latest in a long and distinguished line of Young Widows. It was mostly at our mother people stared, mostly about her they whispered. "She's lovely," people said, nodding their heads, as if that was exactly the right word. Opinion was unanimous that she was "lovely," not "beautiful" or "pretty," but "lovely," implying, it now seems to me, a kind of untouched, even untouchable attractiveness.

They stared because we were still the Divine Ryans, because it was only our fortune that was declining, and not, as people put it, "the family itself." It was as if people believed that our privilege, our status, had nothing to do with money. It was as if they believed that these things were God-given, as if we were simply blessed with them the way that other people were blessed with good looks or intelligence. You could think of the Ryan house, Uncle Reginald had once said, as a kind of giant headstone for which all the Catholics of the city had chipped in, a monument to all the people who had ever read the *Chronicle* or been waked at Reg Ryan's. An audience of customers is what they were, happy customers I hoped, given that Father Seymour's Number was about to perform for them.

As the others took their seats in front, Father Seymour and I went backstage. He began to see to the dancers, who would go on first, while I put on my choir uniform. Before the recital got underway, I peeked out through the curtain. Most of the Catholic dignitaries of the city were in the front row. My mother and Uncle Reginald were sitting together, Mary beside Uncle Reginald, nodding solemnly as he whispered God knows what sort of nonsense to her. Aunt Phil and Sister Louise sat on either side of the archbishop, who would nod his head on the rare occasions when they spoke to him, but did not speak so much as one word in return, only continued to stare with apparent fascination at the empty stage. It was clearly the umpteenth such event that he had attended, and I suspected that he had mastered the art of seeming to watch and listen when in fact he neither had, nor wanted to have, the faintest idea of what was going on. I had seen him sit in just this fashion at every other performance of Father Seymour's Number, staring straight ahead of him. Everyone acted as if the point was not to impress the archbishop, but to refrain from doing anything which would startle him into an awareness of his surroundings.

I watched from the wings as the dance recital got underway. Out came the dancers, all wearing the same look of ingenuous enthusiasm, all smiling at the archbishop as if to watch a group of orphans tap-dancing was known to be the highlight of his year, his favourite pastime. He sat there, still staring straight ahead, wearing that same look of intense concentration, as if he did not want to miss a single click of their shoes. One row came forward as the other went backward, and it went like that as the tempo gradually increased, the dancers tapping faster and faster, the rows interchanging more and more rapidly, coming closer and closer together until, the clicking of their shoes at its height, the dancers formed one row and came to the very edge of the stage, all of them smiling with wide-eyed enthusiasm at his grace, whose head was still at the same angle, so that he now appeared to be staring at their feet, or more accurately at the feet of Young Leonard, who was in the middle. There they were, Father Seymour's dancers, at the very edge of the stage, doing their much-loved running-on-the-spot dance, in which they appeared to be fighting for balance, waving their arms, trying desperately, it seemed, not to fall forwards, though still smiling. Somehow, they moved even closer to the edge, leaned even further forward, smiling more broadly as oohs and aahs came from the audience, smiling as if to say "We're terribly close to falling, aren't we, we're terrible close to falling." (How many boys had been lost, Uncle Reginald asked me later, in practising this manoeuvre?)

The dancers were a huge success. As they left the stage, tap-dancing one by one into the wings, there was a great ovation, the largest for Young Leonard, who was the last to leave, tap-dancing sideways while twirling his green Swiss hat above his head.

Then, after a short intermission during which many of the dancers changed into fresh uniforms, came Father Seymour's choir. I, feeling every bit the fraud and pretender that I was, stood among them, dressed like them, looking just like a real member of the junior choir, even when Father Seymour tapped his baton and the singing began. I stood there, lip-synching "Greensleeves," "Ave Maria," "Barbara Allen," "Sad are the Men of Nottingham."

"Which one is Father Seymour's nephew?" I imagined people in the crowd were asking one another. "Oh he's the one whose mouth is wide open when the rest of them are closed." There was my mother, in the front row, beaming with pride. Looking at her, I was so ashamed that I forgot to move my mouth, but she didn't seem to notice.

I suppose it wouldn't have been so bad if there hadn't been so much talk about my being in Father Seymour's Number. "His own nephew?" I imagined people saying.

"Yes, Draper Doyle is his name. Six months ago, he couldn't carry a note and now look at him."

And there was my mother, to whom the supposed miracle had been meant as a gift, a special favour. Father Seymour takes widow's little boy and makes a special case of him, teaches him to sing in record time. Widow is fairly lifted from her misery by the sight of her boy singing in the chorus of Father Seymour's choir. How guilty I felt! There was my mother, husband-less, sick with worry about me and Mary. Why *couldn't* I be the sort of boy who charmed his mother by singing "Ave Maria?" Why couldn't that pride beaming on my mother's face be justified? What on earth was wrong with me? I was feeling so sorry for myself, I had a sudden urge to burst out bawling, yes, even to confess, right there on the stage, own up to the whole world that I was faking it. Draper Doyle, impostor. I could see the headlines in tomorrow's *Daily Chronicle*, my own family's newspaper. PRIEST'S NEPHEW PRETENDS TO SING WHILE MOTHER BEAMS WITH PRIDE.

Instead of breaking down and confessing, I tried to comfort myself by lip-synching with all my might, belting out the words of "Ave Maria" in my mind, giving what was perhaps the greatest bogus rendition ever given of that song. My mouth was wide open, my shoulders rose and fell with every word. Never had "Ave Maria" been faked more sincerely, more convincingly. I put everything I had into it, straining, straining, sweat breaking out on my forehead, all the while trying desperately not to break down in a fit of shameful weeping on the stage.

It was then, through a glaze of tears, that I saw him. My father was sitting near the back of the hall, at the end of one of the rows. He was dressed as he might have dressed in life for this occasion, wearing his best suit, across the vest of which the gold chain of his watch was visible. He was sitting there, smiling like everyone else, looking not in the least out of place, except that once again he held a hockey puck in his hands. He was turning it over and over as if he was either admiring it or wondering what on earth it was. It might have been something that had fallen from the sky for the way that he was looking at it, now and then tapping it as if to see what it was made of. "Cryptic," his expression seemed to say; "inscrutable," as if the mystery of its origin was as dark and densely opaque as the puck itself.

I looked at the people beside him. Would he show the puck to one of them? He had never appeared this close to other people before. Surely they could see him. Surely, it seemed to me, everyone could see him. He had been as well-known among this crowd as any of the Divine Ryans, so why was his presence not causing a commotion? Why was the person sitting next to him ignoring him as if he wasn't there?

I was determined not to let him get away this time. I knew that with his tendency to disappear in an instant, I had better waste no time in getting to him. He seemed to know what I had in mind, for he looked up from the puck and a mischievous, almost encouraging smile came on his face. To reach the part of the hall in which my father was sitting, I would have to break ranks with the back row of the choir, run clear across the stage, right in front of Father Seymour, then pass within a few feet of Aunt Phil and the archbishop at the bottom of the stairs—after which I would still have to run the length of the hall. Looking once again at my father, whose mischievous expression had become more pronounced, I jumped down from the bleachers we were standing on and, so fast that I didn't notice anyone's reaction, ran across the stage. I was just descending the stairs, just about to reach the floor of the hall, when I glanced up to find that the chair in which my father had been sitting was now empty.

I should simply have kept on going, I suppose, down through the audience and out the door. It wouldn't have been any more difficult to explain. Instead, I came to a skidding halt in front of the archbishop. It was quite a while before the audience realized that what was happening was unplanned. Everyone seemed to think that it was part of the act, some daring innovation of Father Seymour's perphaps, having one of his choirboys run across the stage, descend the stairs and stop in front of the archbishop, there to burst into some spectacular solo for his benefit.

Even Aunt Phil seemed to be hoping desperately that this was the case, hoping the whole thing would suddenly resolve itself into a scene from *Boys' Town*, hoping that somehow I, her nephew, whom she knew to be the newest, least practised member of Father Seymour's Number, would suddenly burst into song, and what had seemed to be a catastrophe would turn out to be one of the great moments in the history of Father Seymour's Number—perhaps it would be remembered as the time that Father Seymour's nephew, on the ingenious instructions of Father Seymour, had fooled everyone into thinking that some horrible embarrassment was taking place, and then had burst into song, his mouth as roundly and as sweetly open as that of some Vienna choirboy, his head gesturing for emphasis, his whole body caught up in serenading the archbishop. For surely, surely, her face seemed to say, I had not simply taken it into my head to flee from the stage and come to a screeching halt in front of his grace.

Not the least of those who must have been expecting some such face-saving performance was the archbishop himself who had been more or less woken up, not by me so much as by the sudden silence, to find that, inexplicably, one of Father Seymour's choirboys was standing right in front of him, staring at him with an expression of simple horror on his face. The archbishop was the first to recover, the first to admit to himself that no serenade, no unprecedented solo would be forthcoming. Smiling at me, he extended his hand, not to shake mine, I was fairly certain, since he did so palm down, but for what reason I had no idea.

Out of the corner of my eye, I saw Sister Louise motioning frantically for me to do something. I saw her rubbing one of her fingers, and making a frantic downward motion with her hands. What this meant, I could not begin to guess. I stared at her in panic, wondering what on earth she wanted me to do.

I dearly wished I understood her, for her expression seemed to assure me that what she had in mind would not only save the moment, but was quite easy to do. When I shrugged, she knitted her forehead, and the motion of her hands became so ferociously concentrated, that her whole body began to shake as if with sheer spite. She was rubbing her finger so vigorously she appeared to be trying to erase her knuckle, all the while staring at me with ever increasing exasperation, as if she believed I was only pretending not to understand. What by this time was obvious to everyone but me was that Sister Louise and the archbishop wanted me to kiss his ring. When it became apparent that I would not, the archbishop lowered his hand, looked away from me, and went back to staring at the stage.

I could think of nothing else to do but turn around and go back onstage, which I began to do, every step of my black buckled shoes resounding throughout the hall. Suddenly, I was acutely aware of my outfit, my elf's hat, my green suspenders, my short pants, the six inches or so of absurdly skinny leg that showed between the pants and my knee-high yellow socks. And finally, the shoes, the famous shoes of Father Seymour's Number in which, one day, if Father Seymour changed his mind about my dancing potential, I might be tap-dancing, footing it about the stage with the same pointless expertise as Young Leonard.

Somehow, Father Seymour got the choir going again and the recital went on as planned, with the audience giving us a kind of bemused, sympathetic ovation at the end. My mother was backstage waiting for me when we went off. Perhaps she had meant to head off the chewing out that I was sure to get from Father Seymour. She needn't have worried. Father Seymour was quite clearly enraged, but he was not about to say anything, for he knew that I might very well blurt out our secret, tell her that, on his instructions, I had only been pretending to sing.

The dressing room was silent as my mother led me out by the hand. When we got to the car, Aunt Phil and Sister Louise had already gone home, so disgusted had they been by my performance. I climbed into the back seat with Mary, and my mother got in front with Uncle Reginald who, saying it might be best if we gave Aunt Phil time to cool off, took us for a drive. For a while, no one but Uncle Reginald spoke. He made the inevitable joke about how, with only three months' training, I had stopped the show. Then my mother turned around.

"I don't suppose," she said, "that you would like to explain yourself." I considered telling the truth, but, remembering my promise to Mary, decided I better not.

"I thought I had to use the bathroom," I said.

"You thought you had to use the bathroom," my mother said. "And then, once you had interrupted everything and spoiled the concert, you discovered that you didn't have to use the bathroom?"

Trying not to mimic her look of incredulity, I nodded.

Mary and my mother looked at one another, rolled their eyes, shook their heads. And then everyone, me included, burst out laughing.

9

BECAUSE OF all the holiday confusion, the next Confession Wednesday was not until three weeks after the concert. In the days before, I tried to think of a way of getting out of it. I could feign sickness, but I would have to seem very sick to convince Aunt Phil to let me miss confession, especially since it was three weeks since we had gone. Mary, who had been genuinely ill, had once asked to be allowed to miss confession and Aunt Phil had assured her that however sick her body might be, her soul was much worse. It seemed there was no end to metaphors when it came to sin. The soul was black. The soul was sick. The soul had too much hair. My normally bald soul would have grown a brushcut's worth of sin in three weeks, so what chance did I have of missing confession? And even if I did miss it, that would only delay the inevitable.

"Bless me, Father, I have sinned. It's been three weeks since my last confession." I repeated those words over and over in my mind, and when Wednesday came, I went to meet my fate, which turned out to be every bit as bad as I thought it would. After reciting some vague infractions of the junior ten commandments, I fell silent.

"Anything else," said Father Seymour. I said nothing.

"Anything else?" he said, somewhat more forcefully than usual, and in the kind of familiar tone he had warned me against using. For a long time, there was silence. The penitent on the other side of Father Seymour, as if to signal his impatience, began to couch. I could faintly hear the shuffle of footsteps from outside, the world, despite my dilemma, going on as usual. I could dimly see Father Seymour, his hand resting on his chin in that reflective pose he always used. I suddenly felt dizzy and fell forward, banging my head against the screen.

"Anything else?" said Father Seymour, who seemed startled. I closed my eyes, remembering my mother's remark that I had "spoiled" the concert.

"I spoiled the Christmas concert," I said.

Without asking for an explanation, he gave me penance.

✦

The visitations continued, as did the Momary nightmares. My father appeared about once a week in the yard next door, dressed for winter as if even ghosts could feel the cold. Once I saw him in the middle of the afternoon, a rare daytime appearance. He stood there in the backyard, holding a puck up to the sunlight like some jeweller appraising a stone, staring at it with one eye closed as if he was trying to see through it, trying to see what it was made of. Later, when I was sleeping, Momary, that strange spectacle of nakedness, pursued me through dreams in which I too was naked. Her object was to get a look at my Methuselah, which I could keep hidden from her only by running as fast as I could, thereby showing her my backside, at the sight of which, in a voice all too like my mother's, she shouted "Look Mary, look, it's Draper Doyle's bum." She was trying to fool me into thinking that to let her see my bum was more humiliating than to let her see my Methuselah, but I wasn't falling for it. I knew it was my Methuselah she was after, and no matter how gleefully she pointed at my bum, I didn't turn around.

I took to sleeping on my back so that when the pee started, when my alarm cock went off, I wouldn't stain the sheet. I was spending all my weekly allowance, as well as drawing from my once-substantial savings, to keep myself in underwear. I wondered if I should ask Uncle Reginald to forgo my oralysis fee, at least for a few weeks, then thought better of it, for he was certain to worm an explanation out of me.

I had visions of becoming like one of those boys we saw in the public health films at school. "Drug addicts will do anything for money," the narrator said, "anything to feed their daily habit." Mine was a weekly habit, one pair of drawers per week on average. My habit. My weekly fix. "The addict begins each day with the knowledge that he must somehow get enough money by nightfall to buy a pair of underwear."

I knew that if I got to the point of spoiling one pair of drawers per day, I was finished. It had gotten so that I could not look at my mother or Mary without thinking of Momary, and therefore of all the underwear I had to buy, as much for their sake as for mine. When I saw Mary, all I could think of was that tuft of hair between her legs, that little goatee which in the dream was always there when I looked over my shoulder—above it was her belly button, her belly like some cyclops with one eye in the middle, coming after me.

I managed to get some revenge on Mary when it came to my attention that she and a boy named Harold Noonan were having what Uncle Reginald called a "fling." A fling was putting it far too strongly since they had yet to speak to one another. All that had really happened was that Harold had taken to following Mary home from school, staring at her from a distance as if he was trying desperately to remember who she was. As for Mary, what strange satisfaction she derived from having a boy to whom she had yet to speak follow her home from school every day, I had no idea. She was always looking back at him, apparently encouraging whatever weird delusion he had formed about her.

Harold Noonan wore shirts with ruffled sleeves, as well as the most bizarrely coloured pants, sometimes red, with purple bell bottoms, sometimes striped. And his hair—combed completely to one side, it was almost as long as Mary's, so long in fact that, to see, he had to walk about with his head turned sideways, sometimes holding his hair in place with one hand while his other hand was in his pocket. He seemed to think that this was a perfectly reasonable way to walk about, a relaxed, self-possessed pose. Sometimes, it looked not as if he was turning his head to keep the hair out of his eyes, but as if that great bunch of hair was pulling his head sideways, so weighing him down that his whole body was thrown off balance, making him lopsided, causing him to walk with one arm much lower than the other, and even with a kind of limp.

There he went, Harold Noonan, looking like someone with a permanent cold in the neck. Aunt Phil, who also noticed Harold Noonan's strange behaviour, called him "That long-haired Lothario from up the street." He was a sight to say the least, that Harold Noonan. I wondered what he would think of Momary. I wondered if, having once seen her, he would still follow Mary home from school.

One day, as Harold Noonan was stalking Mary, I walked along, halfway between them, on the opposite side of the street.

"Go home, Draper Doyle," Mary said.

"Mary, Mary, bum so hairy, how do you make it grow?" I shouted. Mary screamed and began to run—not after me, I was glad to see, but away from me, as fast as possible, her hands over her ears. All Harold Noonan did was feign disinterest.

This episode touched off a renewal of the sex versus age controversy in which Mary and I had been engaging for as long as I could remember. It all hinged on the fact that, while she was three years older than me, I was a boy. She never doubted that those three years would always seem as crucial as they did when we were children, that forty would be as much of an improvement on thirty-seven as nine was on six. Nor did I doubt it, though for a while I did think my age was catching up with hers. It was my father who pointed out that while the difference in our ages would always be three years, the proportionate difference was forever getting smaller. I was faced with the mystery of how, when I was one, she was four times older than me, but when I was two, only two and a half times older. Surely, if my age was an ever-increasing fraction of hers, I told him, it would catch hers some day. My father assured me that this was not even theoretically possible.

My only comfort was that while she would always be older, I would always be a boy. Faced with the fact that most grown-ups of either sex agreed that boys were, as the saying went, "better" than girls, Mary conceded inferiority in sex while trying to convince me that age was more important. She pointed out that she had gone to school before I did, made her first confession and communion before I did, was allowed to stay up later, and so on. I answered that these were things that I would do one day. The mere fact that she had done them first meant nothing. There were, however, things that boys could do that girls could not do at all. I believed that anything that boys could do that girls could not was a blessing, and that anything that girls could do that boys could not was, at the very least, not worth doing and in all probability a curse.

It was, for instance, a blessing to be able to direct your stream of pee in such a way as to explode cigarette butts left floating in the toilet. The thought of the contortions into which Mary would have to twist herself to even come close to accomplishing this feat always sent me into fits of laughter. Then there were things that girls could not do as well as boys. Hockey, for instance. Girls, I informed Mary when I was five, could not play hockey.

Faced with my complete refusal to acknowledge the advantages of being older, Mary had tried to prove her superiority on my terms; that is, on the ice. Though otherwise she was one of those girls who are defiantly incompetent at sports, she was something of a tomboy when it came to hockey. The fact that her sole reason for practising the sport was to beat her brother at it made her unique among the players on Fleming Street, all of whom were boys.

For years, we had played goal against each other, and Mary, to howls of derision from my friends, had often beaten me, though she did so with less and less frequency as time went on. In fact, she had been saying over the summer and fall that she did not want to play against me any more, denying that this decision had anything to do with her recent lack of success.

"I'm too old for playing hockey," she said.

"Too old?" I said. "You're only twelve. Half the Leafs are over forty."

"I think Mary means she's too old for a girl," my mother said. Mary rolled her eyes.

"Too old?" I said. "Mary's too old?" I howled scornfully, knowing that after the Harold Noonan episode she was ripe for a challenge. "C'mon, Mary," I said. "Let's go down to the rink. Me against you."

"Forget it," she said.

"Mary, Mary, bum so hairy," I said, looking at her as if to say that I would complete the sentence if she did not accept. She jumped out of her chair and stood over me, her hands on her hips.

"All right, Draper Doyle," she said, thumping her forefinger against my chest. "All right. I'll play you one last time. ONE LAST TIME. And I'm going to beat you, too."

This was one game that I was determined not to lose. I had the notion that somehow, despite my father's ghost, beating Mary would lay Momary to rest, not to mention keep my alarm cock from going off again. Just the thought of not having to buy any more underwear was inspiration enough. I had lost my spot on the hockey team, I had been shamed into taking my goalie picture down from the wall, all to Mary's glee. It simply would not do for her to win.

We played the following Saturday on the rink at the end of Fleming Street. I enjoyed the usual advantages. While I had every conceivable piece of equipment, including goalie pads and goalie skates and a Habs sweater with Gump Worsley's number on the bank, Mary played goal wearing white figure skates, three overcoats, and copies of *Life* magazine for shin pads. "Mary the Goalie," I called her. On her head, she wore a stocking cap from which her hair hung down, fanning out across her shoulders.

"Got yer pads on, Mary?" one of the boys said, to a chorus of snickers from the others.

"You can see that she doesn't have any pads on," I said, at which the older boys all but fell down laughing. Mary looked at me.

"Shutup, Draper Doyle," she said. "Just please shut up."

We stood at opposite ends of the rink, facing one another. There was Mary, goaded once again into playing goal against me, hoping to beat me the way that she hoped some team, any team, would beat the Habs, and wipe that smirk of invincibility off my face. My defeat was Mary's holy grail, in quest of which she had set out every season for the past five years.

I went to my equipment bag and, throwing aside my trapper, took out the bullhorn which Uncle Reginald had given me for Christmas some years ago.

"No way," Mary shouted. "No way, you're not allowed to use the bullhorn." I held the bullhorn to my mouth and, in a kind of grimly official, we-have-the-house-surrounded tone of voice, said "Yes I am."

"No you're not," Mary said, but my squeakily magnified voice drowned out whatever else she had to say.

"We'll take a vote," I said, speaking through the bullhorn. "Who votes for the horn?" They all raised their sticks except Mary, even the boys on her team. It was universally acknowledged that although to have the bullhorn was an advantage, it made the game more interesting for everyone.

From long practice I had mastered the art of doing a play-by-play commentary even as I was playing goal. "The voice and the goalie of Fleming Street," I called myself. The strange thing was that while I described the play the way that Danny Gallivan would have described it, the bullhorn made me sound like Foster Hewitt. (Foster Hewitt's voice sounded the way anyone's voice would have sounded when magnified by a bullhorn.) I might have been some strange hybrid of the two announcers, possessing Danny's style and Foster's voice.

The game began well for us. In the first five minutes, we scored on Mary twice. The problem was that she was barely able to move in those overcoats; her arms out rigid from her sides, she had to move her whole body when all she really wanted to do was turn her head. Just to keep breathing in those coats, she had to stand fully, exaggeratedly erect, like someone wearing a neck brace. Judging by her height and by the angle at which she was forced to hold her head, I estimated that she lost complete sight of the puck, if not, as some of our team claimed, the moment it crossed centre ice, then certainly when it came to within about ten feet of her. It looked as if she was merely guessing where the puck was, listening for it, her whole body turning one way, then another, her team-mates screaming at her, giving her directions, do this, do that, while Mary tapped about with her goalie stick like someone blind, a look of the most heartrending distress on her face.

Imagine trying to play goal while looking straight up in the air, and you have some idea of how Mary played it. In a goal-mouth scramble, she was helpless. She took pucks in the ankles, sticks on the instep and knees, she slipped on the ice, falling down and struggling in those overcoats to get back up, often falling down again in the process.

As if Mary's problems in the net were not enough, our having the bullhorn gave us a further advantage. I had a way of doing the play-by-play that demoralized the other team. When they had the puck or threw a check, or when Mary made a save, I gave either an understated description of it or none at all. "Mary the Goalie makes the save," I said, or ignored the save she made entirely. But when we had the puck, I described the play the way that Danny Gallivan would: "And Foley comes out with it, ad-libs his way to centre ice and Ohhhh! what a move he puts on Skiffington. He loses it, but Ohhhh! what an enormous body check by Foley."

I used such adjectives as "scintillating" and "larcenous" to describe the saves I made, said that our often dribbling shots were "cannonading," inflated our stickhandling to "a bewildering blur of stick and puck." It amazed me how much effect this sort of thing had on the game, inspiring our players, demoralizing theirs. Despite the fact that we were not playing better than their team, players on both sides were soon convinced that we were. I could see how clearly the other team wanted to hear themselves described as "magnanimous" or "brilliant," and how demoralizing it was for them to hear us described in such terms, even though they knew we didn't deserve it. It was never long before the game began to take on the character of my description, the tone of my voice, our team skating furiously, the other team convinced that we were far better than them, that it was simply not possible for them to beat us.

I hadn't felt so good in a long time. After a long absence, I was back in the net, once again wearing my equipment, and my team was winning. There I was, a goalie stick in one hand, and in the other, not the usual trapper, but a bullhorn which, as it turned out, was almost as good for catching pucks. I doubted that anyone had ever played goal this way before.

"The Bruins look tired, Dick," I said, and sure enough, the other team were soon leaning on their sticks. By this time, the score was 4 – o.

"Four nothing," I said through the bullhorn. "Mary the Goalie looks shaky."

"You're cheating," Mary said, pointing her goalie stick at me. It wasn't enough, she said, that I had the best team, no, on top of that, I had to show favouritism while doing the play-by-play.

It must have been the sight of me catching the occasional puck in the bullhorn that gave her the idea. Just before the game got underway again, she huddled with her team-mates. Then, when the puck was dropped, she screamed "Aim for the bullhorn." The players on the other team who were able to raise the puck abandoned trying to score and began shooting for the bullhorn instead, hoping to either stifle me in mid-voice or bean me with the puck. Soon, I realized that I would either have to stop using the horn or face shot after shot aimed at my head. That puck-shy, choking feeling that had kept me on the bench the year before came back worse than ever. Even though I was wearing a mask and a helmet and was fairly safe from flying pucks, I called time out to throw the bullhorn aside and retrieve my trapper. "Hurray," said the players on the other team.

"Well, Dick," Mary said, "Draper Doyle is having an off day. He's given up the bullhorn and the other team is coming back."

"No way," I said, though my voice, no longer magnified by the bullhorn, sounded so absurdly puny that everyone laughed.

The rest is almost too painful to relate. I no longer had the bullhorn, but I couldn't help thinking that the other team was still aiming for it, aiming for my head. At each shot, I all but turned backwards in the net. In no time at all, the game was tied, and from that point on, it was, as the boys on the other team put it, "all Mary the Goalie." As unlikely as it seemed, she kept making saves, while my vaunted, puck-dodging reflexes kept missing them. The final, shameful, ignominious score was 9 − 4.

"Nine to four," Mary said, pointing her stick at me from the other end of the ice. "Nine to four."

I looked at her, wondering if the colour of my face showed through my goalie mask. The tradition was for the winning goalie to make what was called "One Last Rush" on the other goalie. "It's time for One Last Rush," Mary said. "And this will really be One Last Rush, because I'm not playing anymore after this." This made it that much worse. I could hardly believe it. I had lost the last game that we would ever play. Mary had beaten me for all time.

With the puck in front of her, she stood in goal at one end of the rink while the rest of the players, even those on her team, went to the other end, jamming the ice in front of me, facing Mary. "One Last Rush," Mary shouted, and began to make her way up the ice, all but tiptoeing on those absurd white skates, standing weirdly erect, the overcoats tilting her head at such an angle that she was in danger of falling over backwards, looking like some overstuffed, stick-wielding figure skater, not so much stickhandling the puck as pushing it in front of her, nudging it forward a few feet, then catching up to it and nudging it again. When she reached the halfway point, the rest of the players went out to meet her, skating in what was meant to be slow motion, doing in fact a kind of slow-motion parody of Mary, arms and legs flailing, faces all wearing those agonized expressions we saw in hockey photographs, pretending to try to take the puck from her, only to fail, only to go skating past her as if she had deked them out with some brilliant move.

After they had all been deked out, after they had all gone past her, and there was no one between her and me (I was still standing by myself in the net), they turned around and, catching up with Mary and still moving in a kind of frenzied slow motion, began to grab various parts of her, her shoulders, her breasts, her waist, her arms, some even falling to the ice to wrap their gloves around her skates. None of it was done forcefully enough to pull her down. In fact, they acted as if she was dragging all ten of them along, as if such was her strength that all of them together could not stop her.

They hammed it up, contorting their faces, looking with exaggerated hopelessness at one another, as if she was some superstar whom they could not hope to keep from scoring. I will never forget the sight of those ten boys, almost all of whom were younger and smaller than my sister, their hands just happening to grab her breasts, her backside, her arms, with affected randomness, wrapping about her upper thighs, their faces, as if purely by accident, brushing hers or tangling in her hair. And then there was Mary herself, her expression half mock-heroic, half indignant, as she buckled beneath the weight of the ten peewees who were fastened to her.

Finally, when she had "dragged" them the length of the ice, with ten of them draped all over her, à la Maurice Richard, she started making moves, trying to fake me out of the net. Just as the ten of them began to haul her to the ice in earnest, she deked to the left while I, in accordance with the rules of One Last Rush, made a slow-motion lunge to the right. As the puck went in and as in melodramatic slow motion the boys all fell to the ice, we made "the crowd went wild" noises and Mary landed on her back, her arms upraised, a look that might have been a parody of bliss on her face. Unable to stop, she slid along the ice, knocking my skates out from under me and causing me to fall on top of her, so that my wire goalie mask came to within inches of her face; there we lay, goalie to goalie, two figures so rotund that only about an inch of us was touching, the point of my belly balancing on the point of hers, with a foot-thick wedge of padding between us.

I was so encumbered by my equipment that, when I tried to roll off, I succeeded only in flopping wildly about on top of her, a sight the other boys found so hilarious, they gathered round us in a circle. "Give it to her, Draper Doyle," they said, at which Mary screamed, "Draper Doyle, for God's sake, get off me."

With a manoeuvre she might have been practising for years, she bounced me off her with one thrust of her pelvis. Then she got up and, without a word to anyone, left the rink. Holding her goalie stick on her shoulder, she went clomping up Fleming Street, her white skates making sparks on the pavement. I suspected that few goalies had ever marched so impressively to their retirement.

10

M OMARY DID not appear in my dreams any more frequently after my defeat at Mary's hands, but she was more frightening than before, more witch-like, it seemed to me, pursuing me with outstretched arms, almost close enough to look over my shoulder and see my Methuselah, on which I clamped one hand as I ran. Mary had told everyone of my defeat, but no one had been more tickled by it than my mother, who said she hoped it would teach me a lesson. Uncle Reginald assured me that what he called my "day" was coming, but Aunt Phil took every possible advantage of my low spirits, almost convincing me to write a letter to Father Francis.

One Saturday, not long after what had become known as "the showdown on Fleming Street," I was home by myself when Aunt Phil came back from Reg Ryan's and told me we were "going out."

"Where?" I said.

"Never mind," she said. Taking me by the hand, she led me to the bathroom, where she performed emergency grooming. Standing me on a stool, she bent me backwards over the sink, somehow manoeuvred my head beneath the tap, then turned the water on, the cold water, which matted my hair to my head, so that when she finally released me and had me face the mirror, I looked like some grade-school vampire. She had me put on my blazer and my slacks, then took me by the hand again, leading me out of the house and down Fleming Street.

"Where are we going?" I said. "We're not going to Reg Ryan's are we?" Aunt Phil said nothing.

"Mom said you're not supposed to take me anymore," I said, recalling, as Uncle Reginald put it, that my mother had declared a "moratorium" on wakes.

"Your mother gave me her permission," Aunt Phil said. I tried to pull away from her but she held my hand tighter.

When I thought of all those establishments Aunt Phil might have owned and which I might have had free use of throughout my childhood, the fact that she owned a funeral home was very hard to take. She had been dragging me off to Reg Ryan's since I was five, my parents having not so much approved of her methods as overlooked them. I felt it was entirely possible that I held the world record for most dead bodies seen by a nine-year-old, most time spent in the company of dead people. If it was enough that other boys observe Ash Wednesday once a year, Uncle Reginald once asked her, why did I have to go to wakes once a month? Children, but boys especially, Aunt Phil told him, could never be reminded of their mortality too often.

Aunt Phil believed that men were superior to women, but that, in the very thing that made them superior, lay also the flaw that could destroy them. Men were stronger, yes, but with that strength came pride. It was pride, she said, that had flung Satan headlong from heaven into hell. It was pride that had made a "renegade" of Uncle Reginald who, presumably, had not been to as many wakes as the rest of the family. One way or another, while he was still young enough to reap the benefits, a boy's pride had to be broken. And, for Aunt Phil's money, there was nothing like the sight of a corpse to instil humility in boys.

"I don't want to go," I said, as she dragged me up the street. "I don't have to if I don't want to."

"Nonsense," Aunt Phil said, adding that today's wake, that of a boy about my age, should prove especially instructive. As we walked along Fleming Street, the strange, cold vitality of winter was in the air. It made me shiver.

"How did he die?" I said.

"Who?" Aunt Phil said.

"The boy," I said. "The one we're going to see."

She paused, perhaps to consider which would be more effective, telling me the actual details or letting me make up my own. "Never mind," she said.

It was a rare occasion when at least one of the Divine Ryans was not present at a wake. People expected one of them to be there at all times, Aunt Phil said. Even Uncle Reginald had to take his turn, though he was more or less on call for when the others couldn't make it. I remembered that my father had been as reluctant as Uncle Reginald to take his turn at Reg Ryan's. Luckily, Aunt Phil had preferred not to have him there too often. It was not that she was worried that he would misbehave. Rather, it was what he didn't do while he was there that bothered her. Instead of leading prayers as the others did, or circulating among the mourners, he merely sat or knelt where people could see him.

Which one of the Divine Ryans was sent to sit with you often depended on your social standing. The lesser families rated no better than my father, the least famous, least recognizable member of the family. My father must often have sat at Reg Ryan's among people who had no idea who he was. On one occasion, I had gone with him. As Aunt Phil and I walked along Fleming Street, I could still see my father in the red room, his hat on his knees, enduring the morbid tedium of wakes for his family's sake, sitting there among a crowd of grieving strangers, not knowing what to say to them—half the room staring at him because they knew who he was, the other half staring because they didn't.

He had dreaded what he referred to as the Call, the call to

attend a wake, that is. The Call could come at any time, he told me. It hadn't been so bad before Father Francis had gone to South America. But for the last few years before his death, the Call had been coming more and more frequently. If not for Sister Louise, who spent more time at Reg Ryan's than anyone, who knows how often he would have had to go there? Sister Louise was something of a fixture at the home, her chair almost as familiar a sight in the red room as a casket.

When we reached Reg Ryan's, it was three-thirty. Everyone going into, or even going by Reg Ryan's knew the exact time, for, on top of the sign out front that in bold, black letters read "Reg Ryan's Funeral Home," there was a clock with Roman numerals, a clock that, no matter how disinclined you were to read the sign or to notice the funeral home, you could not help looking at. No one can pass a clock without looking at it, Aunt Phil said, so it was simply good advertising to put one on the sign. That it was also good advertising to put so obvious a reminder of mortality as a clock on the sign for a funeral home, was a fact that went unmentioned.

There were jokes about that clock and Reg Ryan's eagerness to make a dollar. "When time runs out, Reg Ryan runs in," people said. Others said the clock stopped each time someone died; still others that if it stopped while you were looking at it, you would die.

When we went inside and took off our coats and boots in the vestibule, there was no sign of my mother, whom I had hoped might still save me from my fate. Aunt Phil stood behind me, her hands on my shoulders. "Down we go," she said. "And remember where you are." As if I could forget. When we were but halfway down the stairs, I felt it rising up from below, a kind of tangible, wretched silence. I thought I had seen my last wake, but here I was, about to see another one. And what more likely place for my father's ghost to turn up next? I made up my mind that until I reached the casket, where I planned to close my eyes altogether, I would try not to look too closely at anything.

I was glad to discover that today's wake was being held in the blue room, for it was in the red room that my father had been waked, and I had no wish to uncover the still-buried memory of that event. Aunt Phil, her hand on the small of my back, pushed me inside. There was much commotion, much moving aside, as people saw who we were. Despite my determination not to focus on anything, I could not avoid the fact that there, in that sad, dim room, was this gleaming casket. It was almost absurd, the way the white casket outshone the rest of the room, and the mourners, most of whom were dressed in black. White for the innocence of childhood, white though his soul was black with sin and would go to purgatory.

As we neared the casket, I looked at the floor. And as we knelt, I closed my eyes in what I hoped would look to Aunt Phil like fervent prayer. I heard a kind of sibilant murmuring everywhere but in front of me, where I knew the boy was lying. I shut my mind's eye, determined not even to imagine what he looked like.

If Aunt Phil noticed that my eyes were closed, she gave no sign—perhaps she did notice, but dared not say anything. Even when I felt her hand on my shoulder bidding me to stand up, I kept my eyes closed, first turning away from the casket towards where I knew the immediate family was sitting, then rising to my feet. Finally, I opened my eyes to find the dead boy's parents looking at me. That I might remind them of him was something I had not foreseen; no sooner did her eyes meet mine than the woman began to cry, and the man stared wistfully at me.

Then, as if the important thing the day after their son's death was that some stranger not be embarrassed or frightened, they recovered. The woman stopped crying and smiled at me, and the man held out his hand for me to shake. As I took it, I felt so sorry for them I might have started crying had Aunt Phil not put her hands on my shoulders, at which the dead boy's father all but jumped to his feet. He looked as if suddenly the crisis was not that his little boy had died, but that Philomena Ryan was standing in front of him. Aunt Phil bent down and whispered in my ear. "Go sign the book," she said, "then wait for me outside."

I needed no second invitation. I left the blue room and climbed back up the stairs. There were two books at Reg Ryan's. One, which Uncle Reginald called "the Doomsday Book," lay open on a lectern in the vestibule. In this book were recorded the names and the dates of death of people who were waked at the home. On display on a table exactly opposite the Doomsday Book was the Visitors' Book, which all those who attended wakes were asked to sign. We went through two or three Visitors' Books a year, but there had only ever been one Doomsday Book. My father's name was in it, as were the names of all the Ryans who had died since the home had been established. I went to the Visitors' Book and, for the umpteenth and perhaps world-record-setting time for nine-year-olds, signed my name. Aunt Phil was just coming up the stairs when I went outside. Reg Ryan's clock read 4:15.

On our way home, just after we had passed the orphanage, a dog belonging to one of our neighbours began to follow us, running along inside the wire mesh fence that marked his owner's property, barking quite savagely as if we were trespassing. He was a much-feared doberman known on Fleming Street as Tom. His ears were taped up straight above his head—this, according to his owner, was quite usual with dobermans, being the accepted way to "train" their ears. The true doberman, he said, had ears that stood straight up.

The first time I saw Tom, I thought that the tape was some sort of joke, that some brave, foolhardy soul had wrestled him to the ground and somehow managed to tape his ears together. No matter how accepted was this method of training the ears, it made Tom look ridiculous. Because the tape was black, the same colour as his ears, it looked from a distance as if his ears had fused together above his head, as if, far from being the kind of specimen that would win a prize at a dog show, he was deformed. Now, close up, the tape looked like a bandage of some kind, and the erect ears made his head look strangely bare, as if he had just come from having his hair cut. Combine with this the typical doberman expression, that look of vigilant amazement, and you have some idea of what was chasing us.

"Thank God for that fence," Aunt Phil said. No sooner were the words out than Tom leapt up against the fence, his four paws clinging to the mesh and, with his great hind legs lewdly thrusting, he began poking his furry and, it seemed to me, pee-swollen bud through one of the holes, in which it barely fit. What a strange sight it made, Tom with his ears taped up, as if this was somehow necessary to the act, Tom spread-eagled on the fence, looking at us as if we were his inspiration, his furry bud going swiftly in and out, as if it was making repeated attempts to escape, making run after run for it, only to have Tom pull it back.

We could not have been looking at Tom's mad bid for satisfaction for more than one or two seconds when Aunt Phil grabbed me and put her hand over my eyes, my whole face in fact, then proceeded to more or less drag me down Fleming Street. As I stumbled along, trying desperately to get away from her, as much at the thought of how I must look as at the outrage of it, she kept me from falling but said nothing, her hand so firmly on my face that it might have been my mind's eye it was covering, preventing me from even recalling what had

happened, telling me that what I had seen was something that I
must not even think about again, let alone ask questions about.

Only when we were well past Tom's owner's property did
she release me, wordlessly, as if nothing had happened, as if my
face could not still feel the grip of her hand, as if I had not been
wrestled along the sidewalk in broad daylight in what must have
looked to passersby like a kidnapping. For thirty seconds, my
whole face had been stifled by her hand, her one hand, contained by it. But this was a fact that would never be acknowledged between us.

"Aunt Phil," I said, "what was that dog doing?" I knew full
well what her answer would be—it was only to assure myself
that the dog really had existed that I asked.

"What dog?" Aunt Phil said. "There wasn't any dog."

For the rest of the day, I wondered how to tell my mother
about my visit to Reg Ryan's without sounding like a tattletale.
That I had to tell her seemed certain, for I did not want to be
dragged off to wakes once a week for the rest of my childhood.
Before dinner, I kept looking at her, waiting for the right time
to mention it. As it turned out, however, she already knew, for
she had come down to the blue room after we had left and
someone had told her we had been there. After dinner, when I
had all but given up trying to tell her about it, she raised the
subject with Aunt Phil. It was one of the rare occasions when
Aunt Phil looked positively uncomfortable.

"Wakes can do no harm," she said, with eyes downcast. She
and my mother were facing one another across the table.

"Draper Doyle is my child," my mother said. "I've told you
before that I don't want you taking him to wakes and I'm
telling you now. You had no business taking him without my
permission. I'm sure I can trust you not to do it again."

The silence that followed was long and embarrassing for
everyone. My mother had not only spoken sharply to Aunt

Phil, but had done so in front of us. Nor had it been her usual kind of outburst, spoken impulsively one minute and all but retracted the next, but a carefully worded, obviously rehearsed reprimand. Aunt Phil, looking as incredulous as Mary and I, her face blushing deeply, got up from the table and began to do the dishes.

That night, I dreamed that I was in the Forum, on the ice, standing with Aunt Phil in a line of people who, like us, were wearing street clothes. It might have been one of those Depression-era breadlines for the way that we were dressed and the way that we shuffled forward, heads bowed, with no one speaking. Though, throughout the Forum, every seat and inch of standing room was occupied, a kind of church silence hung over everything. There was something naggingly familiar about the scene, but though I tugged on her hand, wanting her to bend down so I could ask her what was happening, Aunt Phil ignored me.

The line was moving slowly towards centre ice where a group of people was standing in a circle, as if some sort of pre-game ceremony was underway. Some of the people in the line were holding candles, others flowers. I saw each one of them enter the circle, then emerge, seconds later, empty-handed, to rejoin the line on the other side of centre ice. The line stretched from one end of the ice to the other, people coming in through a gap in the boards at one end and leaving through a gap at the other end, pausing only within the circle to leave their candles or their flowers.

When we drew close to the circle, a strange whispering began among the crowd. I strained to listen and discovered that everyone in the Forum was whispering "Morenz."

"Morenz." The very name seemed full of death. I now realized what was happening. It was exactly as Uncle Reginald had once described it to me. Aunt Phil was taking me to see the great Howie Morenz, who was being waked at centre ice. Morenz was the fastest skater who had ever lived, or ever died for that matter, for his speed had killed him. Morenz had died in 1937, only a few weeks after crashing into the boards at the Forum and breaking his leg. No one knew exactly what killed him, but it was said that after being told that the broken leg would mean the end of his career, he had lost the will to live.

Morenz was Uncle Reginald's favourite among the Habs, as much because his funeral had been held at centre ice in the Montreal Forum as because he had been a great hockey player. "The ultimate funeral," Uncle Reginald called it, the Forum filled with twenty thousand people, all come to say goodbye to Morenz whose open casket lay at centre ice almost buried in flowers. After the funeral, the casket was drawn by horse and carriage through the city streets which were lined with people, many of whom had been turned away from the Forum, and had waited for hours to catch a glimpse of the funeral as it went past. How he would have liked to have worn his top-hat in that procession, Uncle Reginald said, to have driven the horse and carriage that took Morenz to his final resting place.

I felt less afraid, now that I knew where we were. Aunt Phil and I were taking part in one of the greatest moments in Habs history. "Morenz," the crowd kept whispering. "Morenz," I said, as the circle slowly broke to let us in. There in front of us, laid out in what might have been a bed, with a blanket of flowers pulled up to his chin, was the great Morenz. As we moved towards the casket, the whispering grew louder, as if something especially momentous was about to happen. "Morenz," they said, as if the first rumours of his death had just begun—the very name was like a moan, a sigh of grief.

I was surprised to see that Aunt Phil was crying. When we reached the casket, she stood behind me, then put her hands beneath my arms and lifted me. I looked around at the circle of mourners, suddenly realizing that all of them were members of my family. Aunt Delia, whom I'd only seen in photographs, was there with Uncle Reginald. Father Seymour and Father Francis were standing on either side of Sister Louise, who held, in one clenched fist, a set of black prayer beads. My mother was there, her arms around Mary who was staring at me.

"Kiss him," Aunt Phil said. "Kiss the man goodbye." She began to lower me towards the casket.

"Kiss him," Aunt Phil said.

I looked down to see, not Morenz, but my father, his hair slicked back, a kind of spectral handsomeness about him, my dead father, waiting for a kiss from the one person who could bring him back to life.

"Kiss him," Aunt Phil said.

"No!" I screamed, "No!" as she lowered me towards him. Closer came my father's face, closer, until soon the dream was nothing but his face, a great, looming death mask.

"Kiss him!" Aunt Phil shouted, all but dropping me on top of him. I turned aside at the last second so that we did not so much kiss as bump faces, my forehead nudging his cold cheek, jiggling his flesh in a way I could still feel when I woke up screaming.

11

OF ALL THE sessions of oralysis I had with Uncle Reginald, the ones I liked best, the ones that came closest to being worth the fifty cents I had to pay for them, were the ones he collectively called "The Mid-season Review." For several weeks in a row we talked about hockey, about how the Habs were doing, what their chances looked like for a third straight Stanley Cup. The biggest obstacle, Uncle Reginald said, would likely be, not our nemesis, the Leafs, than whom there had never been an NHL team more aged, more decrepit, or less talented, but the Chicago Black Hawks, led by the Golden Jet, the awesome Bobby Hull, in whose massive shadow the entire league was playing. The Black Hawks were in first place, an incredible fifteen points ahead of Montreal, who were barely keeping pace with the Leafs and the lowly Rangers. Montreal, Uncle Reginald said, would have to find a way to stop Hull, who once again, was well on his way to scoring fifty goals.

The favourite phrase of the colour commentators that year was "You can't stop what you can't see." They used it whenever Bobby Hull wound up for a slapshot. That's all people talked about, the speed of Bobby Hull's shot. How fast was it? people wondered. During oralysis, Uncle Reginald solemnly informed me that Bobby Hull's slapshot was faster than the speed of light. Hull's shot, said Uncle Reginald, was so fast that it went backwards in time, so that Hull was literally rewriting the record books, scoring goals, not only in the present but in the past, changing the outcome of games played thirty, forty, fifty years ago. This is how Uncle Reginald imagined Montreal's colour commentators, Dick Irvin Jr. and Danny Gallivan, talking about Hull's shot:

"We've just gotten word, Danny," Dick said, "that Hull's last slapshot, the one that disappeared at the blueline in the second period, turned up in the Stanley Cup Final of 1965, April 17 to be exact, a game which the Habs won 3 − 2, but which has now been tied up 3 − 3 by Hull's blistering slapshot and is going into overtime. Habs fans will recall that the Habs won that series in seven games, which means that, if the Hawks should win in overtime, the Cup for 1965 will go to them."

"I bet I can guess where Hull's slapshot is going," said Danny Gallivan.

"You betcha," said Dick. "Right back to 1965. I hope the Gumper is ready."

"I pity Gump Worsley," said Danny. "Those slapshots from the future must be almost impossible to stop."

"Definitely," said Dick. "I mean, how do you cut down the angles on a shot that won't even be taken for another two years?"

"If anyone can do it, the Gumper can," said Danny.

I loved the notion of Gump Worsley, who was so indignant when his defencemen allowed so much as one shot from the present, having to stop shots from the future, the Gumper standing in his net, watching the play at the other end of the ice, when suddenly from out of nowhere a puck appears at the blueline, a small black blur from the future, Bobby Hull's time-travelling, 1967 slapshot, which, unless it is stopped by the Gumper, will win the Cup for 1965. I tried to imagine the expression on the Gumper's face as pucks from both the present and the future came flying at him. After being scored on, he would likely take the puck and, with his goalie stick, bat it baseball-fashion into the stands. Then he would turn and, with his monkey face beet red and his big ears sticking out, demand an explanation from his defenceman. Bobby Hull's time-travelling slapshot. What chance would the Habs have against it?

Through the coldest month of winter, with the fire-escape steps treacherous with snow and ice, Uncle Reginald still forbade me to use the lift. Not that I minded. Each afternoon, as I made my way up four flights of steps, sometimes in the darkness, I wished there was nothing else to think about but hockey, no reason to go to Uncle Reginald but to hear him talk about the Habs. After each session of oralysis, however, the same old problems were always waiting for me. There was, for instance, the ever-deepening problem of Father Seymour and my supposed membership in the Number.

It wasn't until February that Father Seymour had me spar with one of his Number. Or should I say that it wasn't until February that he had one of his Number hit me in the face, for there was no sparring. Father Seymour paired me with Young Leonard, an unlikely opponent for a beginner it seemed to me, though I didn't say so. Young Leonard's first punch hit me squarely on the nose. Eyes watering so badly that I couldn't see, I backed away from him, trying—it must have looked quite ridiculous—to wipe my eyes with my boxing gloves. No one took much notice of me until Father Seymour came running from the other side of the gym. He put his arm around me, then put his face up close to mine, moving about this way and that as if I was trying to hide behind the gloves.

"Draper Doyle," he said, as if he was embarrassed for me, "Draper Doyle, you're not crying, are you?"

"No," I said, genuinely surprised at the very suggestion. I dropped my gloves and, through eyes still badly watering, looked at him. As if to say that I was the very picture of crying, he smiled and, still with his arm around me, told me that I could go home if I wanted to. By this time, the whole gym had gone silent and all the boys were watching.

"I'm not crying," I shouted at him, now so self-conscious that my eyes began to water even more freely than before.

"All right," he said, "all right, you're not crying," then magnanimously turned his back, as if I obviously was crying and his only concern was to spare me further humiliation.

The truth was that I felt like going home, but I knew that if I left now, I would have to ask him to unlace my boxing gloves, there being no one else in the gym whose hands were free. The thought of standing there, in the middle of the gym, eyes streaming tears, holding out my arms while he unlaced my gloves and all the other boys watched, was less appealing than going back to sparring with Young Leonard, which I decided to do, only to find that Young Leonard, no doubt at some signal from Father Seymour, had paired off with one of the other boys. I was relieved to see that some of the younger boys were doing laps around the gym. When they came round to where I was standing, I fell in with them and somehow managed to keep running until practice was over.

Father Seymour never again paired me with Young Leonard. In fact, it was only on rare occasions that he had me spar with anyone, and only then with boys who were much smaller than I was, boys so small that to hit them or be hit by them would have been humiliating, so I avoided both, keeping them at arm's length or throwing my arms around them in a kind of hug. Father Seymour focussed his attention on the older boys, never actually coaching me or any of my pint-sized opponents on how to box. I presumed that, as with the choir and tap-dancing practice, he had given up on me, deeming me to be a waste of time that would be better spent coaching boys who had at least a chance of winning at the tournament in March.

The strappings continued, though I had yet to be his victim. Often when he finished strapping one of the boys, he would smile at me, though what he was trying to tell me by doing so I had no idea. Was it that I was exempt from strapping because I was his nephew, or was the notion that I was exempt supposed to be a kind of private joke between us? It was clear that he believed that we had an understanding of some kind, but I could not decide what it was.

How relieved I was each day when he blew his whistle to end the practice. While Father Seymour and the other boys went back to the orphanage, I walked home alone. I was glad to leave that place at five o'clock, not to have to go to the orphanage like the other boys, not to have to eat, night after night, in the great hall, with the pictures of all those orphans who had gone on to become Christian Brothers looking down at me.

Outside, it was always very cold. In the light from the streetlamps along Fleming Street, I could see my breath, trailing out behind me in great plumes of frost. None of the people watching from the houses along the street knew that Young Leonard had hit me in the face, or that my eyes had watered so much that Father Seymour had been able to pretend that I was crying, or that he now had me fighting boys from a faction of the Number known as "the pygmies." To them, I was just someone heading home on a cold night, someone who, hunched as I was into my duffle coat with my hands in my pockets, made them glad to be indoors where it was warm.

For some reason, this thought always made me feel warmer. I would take the long way home, starting from the other end of Fleming Street, going past *The Daily Chronicle*, as well as the outdoor rink, so I could see how the ice was doing and, somewhat morbidly perhaps, relive my defeat at Mary's hands.

Each time I passed the *Chronicle*, I thought of the photograph on Aunt Phil's mantelpiece. On the mantelpiece in Aunt

Phil's living room, framed, hinged together, looking like an open book, there stood two photographs of my father. In the left photograph, he was standing on the sidewalk in front of the *Chronicle* wearing his newspaper bag, the strap of which ran like a sash across his chest. In the right photograph, taken fifteen years later during his first day as editor of the *Chronicle*, he was standing in exactly the same place, this time wearing his editor's cap which my mother had bought for him and which, except to pose for that photograph, he had never worn.

The two photographs seemed to tell a story, to bracket the formative years of the kind of self-made man that each of my grandfathers had been. In the missing middle, there might have been the classic climb to success—from paper boy to mail boy to printer's helper to proof-reader to reporter to desk editor to editor, all in fifteen years. In both photographs, my father was smiling, the boy and the man smiling at each other, it seemed, except that in the second photograph, he was smiling as if he knew the joke, as if he could already see himself on the mantelpiece, paired with his younger self, the paper boy.

There had been twenty priests at my father's funeral, Uncle Reginald told me. I doubted that the death of a fellow priest would have drawn so many. The sight of so many priests around the casket had caused more than one person to recall how, at one time, my father had planned to be a priest himself. After his graduation from high school, he had surprised everyone with his announcement. He had shown no inclination whatsoever in that direction while growing up. It had been presumed that "bookish" as he was, he would take over the *Chronicle* one day, become what Sister Louise called "the family's man of letters." My father had wanted to enter the priesthood, but his father, irony of all ironies, had prevented him from doing so.

At this point, Father Francis and Father Seymour were already in the seminary, and Uncle Reginald, ten years married, had no children. It had looked like what Uncle Reginald called "the Ryan Line" would end unless my father accepted marriage as his vocation. Reg Ryan Sr. used his considerable influence among the city's priesthood to make sure that none of them even considered my father for the seminary. There was apparently some bitterness between father and son for a time, but this had passed when Reg Ryan Sr. agreed to the compromise of sending my father to Oxford to pursue a layman's course in Latin and scholastic philosophy. The implication of the story seemed to be that these scholarly interests were the real reason my father had wanted to join the priesthood, and that marriage was therefore no great sacrifice for him to make.

It would be going too far, but only just too far, to say that my parents' marriage had been arranged. It was more, Uncle Reginald once told me, like they were "recommended" to each other. I was hardly more likely to think of them as a couple than I was to think of Uncle Reginald and Aunt Delia as one. Aunt Delia, whom I could not remember, had died six years ago. I could not imagine Uncle Reginald ever having been married, his strange life joined to someone else's. But neither could I imagine my father's life ever having been joined to someone else's.

I remembered that there had been a curious awkwardness between my parents, especially on my father's part, right up to the time he died. Eight years into marriage, and his family was still coaching him on how to act towards his wife and still explaining him to her, making jokes about habits of his that she would have to get used to as if they still knew him far better than she did. They might have been just married or might have just announced their engagement for the way that the family carried on. At Christmas or on birthdays a public kiss had always been required. "Give her a kiss, Donald," Sister Louise would say teasingly, as if, like schoolyard sweethearts, they were too embarrassed to admit their affection for one another.

Everyone would watch and applaud as my father kissed my mother, my mother trying to disguise the fact that she had to incline her head for him to reach her, my father standing awkwardly on tiptoe, his hands on her shoulders.

It was more than the standard busybody inlaws treatment, for it was carried to such extremes that even my father complained from time to time, though only to my mother, who would tell him to speak to them about it, at which point he would drop the matter. There seemed to be a feeling that the inlaws could not, in fact must not, leave Donald to his marriage, that there was no telling what would happen if they were not there to keep him from making mistakes, or when he made them, to explain them to his wife. One or another of them was always on the phone to her, coming to see her while he was at the newsroom, making allowances for him, encouraging her to share their view of him as a hopeless eccentric whom no one person could possibly take care of, much less understand.

He was a kind of hobby that all members of the family shared. Her marriage had won her a free, lifetime membership in the Donald club, the mystified-by-Donald club, the what-on-earth-will-Donald-do-next club, the save-Donald-from-himself club, whose members were cheerfully dedicated, not only to taking care of Donald, but to trading stories about him, "Donald stories," as Sister Louise called them. Of course, my mother had more Donald stories than anyone else, at least more new ones, so it was usually she that told them and the others who listened. Aunt Phil, Father Seymour, Father Francis, Sister Louise, all listened to the supposedly just-for-fun Donald stories with such grave expressions on their faces that our mother finally realized that she was their way of keeping tabs on him and stopped telling Donald stories altogether.

Every day after boxing practice while I was going past *The Daily Chronicle*, I thought of my father taking this same route

home at four in the morning, walking by himself down Fleming Street. Sometimes at four or five o'clock in the morning,
after a sixteen-hour shift at the *Chronicle*, instead of going
home he would go down to the rink and, to the disbelief of
the people who lived nearby and who, even with their windows closed, could hear him, he would go skating for half an
hour. More than one of the neighbours, perhaps after failing to
get satisfaction from him about the matter, had complained to
our mother. Why, they wanted to know, was a grown man out
skating by himself at four in the morning while others tried to
sleep?

One day, as I was walking home, I heard it, the unmistakable sound of someone skating. Long before I reached the rink,
I knew it was my father. I began to run and by the time I got
there he was skating hard, head down. He was wearing his
duffle coat, the hood of which was up, and his flannel slacks,
which the wind was blowing against him, outlining his thin,
somehow pathetic legs.

I watched from Fleming Street as, by himself, oblivious to
all else, he skated around the darkened rink, bent over from
the waist as if there was nothing in all the world but that stretch
of ice in front of him. He seemed to be constantly picking up
speed, not even slowing down to take the turns, but using
them to gain momentum. His fur-lined hood gave him a kind
of phantom look as he went around the rink so fast it seemed
his skates were barely making contact with the ice. It was as if
he was making progress towards some goal, working up to
some speed, perhaps, that in his lifetime he had been unable to
achieve.

I went closer to the boards, waiting for him to come down
the wing again, squinting into the darkness to make him out, to
make sure that it was him. At the far end of the rink, he made
his turn, then shot out of it towards me, coming straight at me,

emerging from the darkness with both arms swinging, his duffle coat squeaking in time to the sound his skates were making. For the barest fraction of a second, as he was going past me, he looked up, his eyes staring in what might have been wide-eyed amazement, as if it was me who had come back from the dead to watch him skate.

"Dad!" I screamed, as he turned to avoid crashing into the boards. Without so much as slowing down, he went back up the other wing, and disappeared in a flurry of arms and legs into the darkness, this time for good, for there was sudden silence. I jumped over the boards and, getting down on my hands and knees, began searching the ice for the marks my father's skates had made. The rink must have been flooded just after dark, for there were no marks on the ice except his. I imagined throwing a huge sheet of paper over the ice, then shading it to find the patterns he had left behind. I could take it home to Uncle Reginald, roll it out for him in the backyard like some giant shroud, an image in negative of my father's presence in the world. But it was an image visible to me alone, for I knew that, even if I were to bring people to the rink and show them the skate marks, I could not prove that it was my father who had made them.

I lay down on the ice on my back, spreading out my arms and legs. Looking up at that clear cold February sky, I remembered something my father had once told me, a variation on that old idea that what we call stars are really holes in the sky with the light of heaven shining through them. A star, my father said, was a hole made when a puck had been punched out of the night sky. All pucks came from the sky, he said. And the end of the world would come when there was no sky left.

I wasn't sure I liked the idea that if not for hockey, the world would last forever, that with each puck that went flying into the stands or was otherwise lost, the world took one more step towards oblivion. On the other hand, for a few weeks at least, it had made playing goal more interesting. The thought that the puck might have been a little fragment of time itself gave added meaning to the notion of making a save. I would pretend that I was trying to stop the puck, not from going into the net, but from flying off into oblivion. I concocted elaborate fantasies in which the continued existence of planet earth depended on my skill as a goaltender. There I was, standing bravely with my back to oblivion, trying to keep time itself from getting past me, defending the world against those agents of time, those ever-advancing forwards. I had even had a nightmare in which a great deluge of pucks was falling from the sky— the "Apuckalypse," my father called it when I told him about it.

I looked up now at all the stars, the puck holes through which the light of eternity was shining down. Then the way that I was lying on the ice, with my arms and legs spread out, reminding me of something else my father had said, not long before he died. He asked me if I had ever heard of the expression "fire on ice." I told him I hadn't. "Some people call hockey fire on ice," he said. We talked for a while about the aptness of this description. Then he put his hands on my shoulders. "But do you know what else it means?" he said. I shook my head. He reminded me of the picture in the *Cartoon Dante*. It showed, at the bottom-most pit of Dante's hell, at the very core of the Inferno where the fires of retribution should have been most intense, a solid block of ice. And within that block of ice, frozen for all eternity, caught forever in the act of committing mortal sin, lay Satan—a figure of perfect isolation, utter loneliness, his arms and legs spread-eagled, his eyes staring up through the ever-widening circles of hell to heaven, where the saved were looking down at him with scorn.

I had told Uncle Reginald about my father's strange story. "The Fire On Ice Sermon," he called it, assuring me that

Satan's name did not appear even once in the NHL's official book of rules and regulations.

Why my father had told me the story, I had no idea. Lying there on the rink, spread-eagled on the ice like some tiny Satan, I began to shiver. Closing my eyes, I folded my arms for warmth. I heard the wind rushing through the trees along the street. Night, puck-black night, in all its immutable aspects, was coming down.

12

S OMEONE IN Father Seymour's Number must have let slip
that I had only been lip-synching at the Christmas concert,
for Aunt Phil, saying that she didn't want my mother to hear
about it first "on the street," told her everything. That is, she
put the best face possible on the matter, at least where Father
Seymour was concerned. The whole thing had been done for
her sake, Aunt Phil told her, to spare her the disappointment
and the embarrassment of finding out that not even Father Seymour could teach her little boy how to sing. The problem, her
tone implied, was not that I had had no talent, but that I had
been wilfully obtuse, resisting Father Seymour at every step.

"Them that will not learn cannot be taught," said Sister
Louise.

The only one of the Divine Ryans not present when my
mother was informed of what Uncle Reginald called "The
Christmas Concert Caper" was its master-mind, Father Seymour. He even missed confession the following Wednesday, so
that ten days passed before he and my mother spoke again, at
which time not one word was said about the matter. In fact, the
two of them went to great lengths to avoid looking at each
other. It was obvious that despite Aunt Phil's defence of his
motives, she and Sister Louise were disappointed with him, a
fact of which Father Seymour was only too aware. So nervous
he could not sit still, he fell even further in their eyes by pacing
back and forth in the living room, now and then peering

through the drapes as if he might have to leave at any moment. Aunt Phil and Sister Louise watched him with such evident disapproval that it's little wonder he blurted out what he did.

"Will you be coming to see him box?" said Father Seymour, his hands behind his back, looking first at me and then at my mother as if to say "Has Draper Doyle mentioned the matter yet?"

"Oh, I—of course," my mother said, "of course. Draper Doyle never said—"

"We're fighting United next week," said Father Seymour, smiling at me in a way which seemed to fondly recall many days spent together in the gym, preparing for United. He might just have mentioned some secret and soon-to-be-unveiled masterpiece for the way that Aunt Phil and Sister Louise lit up, beaming at him. "Here, finally, is Father Seymour," their expressions said.

The whole thing was so absurd, I had a kind of perverse and barely resistible urge to play along with it, to say something about how eagerly I was looking forward to the tournament. What I should have done was expose him for a fraud, then and there, but I didn't. Everyone seemed so pleased with me, not to mention relieved that something was soon to happen that would make us all forget the Christmas concert.

What on earth Father Seymour was thinking of I did not find out until the next day in the gym, when he informed me that contrary to "our" original plan, I would be taking part in the tournament.

"But I haven't got a chance," I said. "I can't box."

"It doesn't matter if you lose," said Father Seymour, and before I could tell him that on the contrary, it mattered a great deal to me, he added "The important thing is that you take part, that's all."

"Why?" I said.

"It just is, that's all," he said.

He assured me that I had nothing to be afraid of, for I would fight a boy at my own "skill level." I doubted very much that such a boy existed, and I said so, pointing out that my only boxing experience to date was a few sparring matches with Young Leonard, which had ended either with water running from my eyes or blood running from my nose.

"Don't worry," he said. "The boy you'll fight won't be as good as Young Leonard." This was not saying much, given that no one was as good as Young Leonard.

That night, I kept mentioning my upcoming bout, hoping my mother might object to it, but she didn't. As far as she knew, I had been practising for the past six months, and would no doubt fight a boy my age and size who had also been practising that long. The fact that I had been coming home from practice looking none the worse for wear must have further reassured her that Father Seymour had been taking proper care of me.

I wondered if I should swallow my pride and confess to everything, but I couldn't do it. Having been caught in the Christmas concert hoax was bad enough. I remembered the look on her face when Aunt Phil told her that I was faking it. She was not, as Aunt Phil would have it, disappointed because I had failed, but because I had lied to her—so disappointed, in fact, that she could not bring herself to speak to me about it. Nor could I bring myself to tell her that even my membership on the boxing team was a hoax. And quite aside from how she would react, there was no telling what Father Seymour would have done.

"Could you ask Father Seymour," I said, "to let Uncle Reginald be in my corner?"

She promised me she would, and the next day told me that Father Seymour had agreed, provided that Uncle Reginald "stayed out of the way" and let him do the coaching. When I asked Uncle Reginald to be my corner man, he said he would be honoured, so it was settled.

✦

There had always been someone like Young Leonard in Father Seymour's Number. The little fireplug. The inspirational half-pint. The boy you suspected or at least hoped was secretly despised by everyone. Boys like Young Leonard were there to guarantee the moral victory. They were so small that just to step into the ring with them seemed an act of cowardice. By the way we booed Young Leonard's opponent the night of the tournament, you'd have thought it was he who had arranged for Young Leonard to be there, and not us. For Father Seymour, a fight was not really "won" unless a moral victory came with it. The point was not so much to win as to make the other fighter so resentful of your skill, of your ability to hit him in the face, that he would resort to unfair tactics.

The point in other words was to goad him into cheating, so that you not only won the fight but came away with a moral victory as well. When, from sheer spite, Young Leonard's opponent started "cheating," that is, clutching, pushing, throwing low blows, Father Seymour assumed a confident "virtue shall prevail" expression; on the one occasion that Young Leonard took a punch, he assumed an "even if we lose we win" expression. At no time did he complain about the tactics the other boy was using, nor did our team. We all just sat there, watching, waiting for our own fights to begin. Only the Catholics in the crowd complained. It was not enough that Young Leonard's opponent was twice the size of Young Leonard, their booing seemed to say—no, he had to cheat as well. Being bigger was unfair, breaking the rules was unfair, but for some reason possessing ten times as much skill as your opponent was not unfair. Skill was a measure of virtue, it seemed.

Abandoning even the pretence of boxing, the other boy grabbed hold of one of Young Leonard's legs and tried to wrestle him to the canvas; when that didn't work, when Young Leonard somehow managed to keep his balance, the other boy tried, still holding the leg, to throw Young Leonard through the ropes. Young Leonard looked as if this leg-grabbing was the standard desperation move of his opponents, one he had encountered many times before; he hopped around with such apparent ease on one leg that, when the referee pulled him away, the other boy, on hands and knees on the canvas, was almost weeping with frustration. A great cheer went up. Young Leonard had done it again. The fight was called and Father Seymour, with a kind of "gloating is beneath me" look about him, wordlessly escorted Young Leonard from the ring.

It went on like that, the boys of Father Seymour's Number so embarrassing and irritating their opponents with their combination of skill and self-righteous good sportsmanship that most of United was disqualified for cheating, for flailing away with low blows that had such little effect on the boys of Father Seymour's Number that the Protestant fans began making remarks about what was done with choirboys to make them better boxers. Once, one of our Number, Terry O'Shea, did go down after receiving a low blow; when the fight was called and Father Seymour led him from the ring, Terry was still doubled over, but so determined was he not to let the agony he was feeling register on his face, he had a kind of half-impassive, half-stricken look about him, like that of someone trying to set a world record for holding his breath; his wistfully unfocussed eyes were blinking rapidly, but his unwavering dedication to the cause, his willingness to make the supreme sacrifice was evident in the way the muscles of his bloodless face were clenched.

In this, he seemed to say as Father Seymour led him, doubled over, past his gleeful detractors, in this mastery of my facial muscles lies your defeat.

It was a stirring display of willpower, to say the least, one I was quite certain I could never duplicate, though I might well have the opportunity. In fact, my sympathies, as I climbed into the ring, were entirely with the other side. The moral scorecard read 9 – 0 by the time I set eyes on my opponent, a boy who, I was glad to see, looked to be every bit as puny and disinclined to punch and be punched as I was. Father Seymour had been as good as his word, it seemed, for here was a boy who was almost as much of a weakling as I was.

A great cheer went up when my name was announced. Most of the people there, half of whom were Catholics who had been following Father Seymour's boxers for years, believed, presumed that I could fight, that I was a bona fide member of Father Seymour's Number and that the other boy was therefore the underdog. No one believed it more than the other boy himself, who was quite clearly trying to hide the fact that he was terrified, looking at me with such transparently affected scorn that I felt sorry for him. I gave him what was intended to be a reassuring smile which so unnerved him that he turned around. "C'mon, Jeffie," shouted a man in the crowd, his voice so pleadingly sorrowful he could only have been Jeffie's father. I was glad that, at the last minute, my mother and Mary had decided not to come.

As I stood in my corner, Father Seymour gave me no instructions whatsoever—not that this was unusual. He never gave any of his fighters instructions, only stood there behind them as if to say that to give fighters of their ability instructions would have been entirely superfluous, as if nothing could make them more ready than they already were. That, for different reasons, instructions would also have been superfluous in my case, no one but me, my team-mates, and Father Seymour knew. Even Uncle Reginald didn't know, for I hadn't had the nerve to tell him. It occurred to me, however, that Father Seymour's silence must be conveying the wrong impression to the boxing fans assembled. I peered into the crowd, and sure enough, people were staring at me as if I was doubtless a boxer of sinister, if not immediately apparent, abilities. They seemed to find my puniness especially intriguing—was I, their expressions seemed to say, another Young Leonard, a brawling fury cunningly disguised as a weakling?

Uncle Reginald had bought me a terry-towel bathrobe, onto which he had sewn my name, "Draper Doyle Ryan." (Mary's "half-an-orphan" joke had by this time gotten round the city. Why, some of the Protestants wanted to know, did half an orphan need two names?) This only made matters worse, for it was assumed that any boxer who had his own bathrobe must be terrific. "That robe won't help ya when the fight starts," shouted the boys from the other school, who were obviously convinced that I would win in the first thirty seconds.

Then there was the imposing figure of Uncle Reginald, standing in my corner. Unlike Father Seymour, he was shouting instructions, chattering away as if he had memorized the words in some boxing manual without bothering to find out what they meant. He kept telling me to follow the left jab with the left uppercut which, as far as I could see, would have been impossible even for someone who knew how to box, let alone for someone who didn't. On top of everything, there was the name of Ryan on my bathrobe, a name which the Catholics in the audience would expect me to do proud and which the Protestants despised—surely any nephew of Father Seymour, any Divine Ryan, was a young man to be reckoned with.

Had I not been wearing my mouthpiece and my headgear, I might have set about lowering their expectations, running around to all four corners of the ring, preparing the audience for disappointment, assuring everyone that I couldn't box, disarming the hatred of the Protestants who were looking at me with a kind of begrudging admiration, as if it was inevitable that one of their boys fall victim to me and all they asked was that he land at least one punch. "I am Draper Doyle," I felt like telling them, "owner of the known universe's least hairy, most wrinkled Methuselah. I do not know how to box."

At last, the bell rang, and my opponent and I touched gloves. It occurred to me that this might be the last glove that I would lay on him. For a while, as Uncle Reginald said later, the element of surprise was on my side. The other boy was so surprised at how badly I was fighting that sometimes he forgot to hit me. He looked darkly puzzled, as if he suspected that letting him hit me was part of some sinister strategy of mine—perhaps I was one of those boxers who needed to be hit a dozen times before his anger was aroused.

Each time I got hit, Uncle Reginald shouted "That's it, Draper Doyle," which must have added to the boy's confusion. It certainly added to mine. The other boy really wasn't very good—any of our other boxers would have had him cheating by the second round. But he was good enough to block my pitiful attempts at punching and find a way around my pitiful attempts at blocking.

The first round was almost over before the crowd, the Protestant part of it especially, began to realize what was happening. When the bell rang, the Protestants sent forth a rousing cheer for Jeffie. The voice I had taken to be that of Jeffie's father was loudest, shouting "Good round, Jeffie, good round," as if he dared not to hope too much, as if there was still a chance that one round was a fluke and the awful beating would happen in the second. Others, who knew boxing better or whose judgement was not skewed by having a relative in the

ring, were quite certain that I was already beaten. A lot of
Protestants remarked on the appropriateness of my having an
undertaker in my corner.

"If yer dyin', see Reg Ryan," said the Protestants.

"C'mon choirboy," the Catholics said, which usually fired
up the pride of any member of Father Seymour's Number, for
it was as good as asking him to fight for his religion and his
people. "C'mon now, choirboy," they said. "Ya gotta take it to
him in the second round."

As I sat down in the corner, Uncle Reginald rubbed my
shoulders and Father Seymour just stood there, still saying nothing but looking very worried.

"What about it, Seymour?" said Uncle Reginald. "What's
our strategy?"

"No strategy," said Father Seymour, trying to look as if
the whole thing had been planned or at least foreseen. "Neither
of the boys can box," he said, "so there's not much I can tell
Draper Doyle."

"Keep your gloves up, Draper Doyle," said Uncle Reginald,
tossing his head in disgust at Father Seymour as the bell rang to
start the second round.

After taking about thirty seconds of an ever more furious
beating, it occurred to me, quite irrationally I now realize, that
I should try smiling at my opponent again. In fact, dizzy from
the blows that I had received, giddy from the pain in my head
and my stomach, I for some reason felt like smiling. It even
occurred to me, without in the least seeming absurd, that smiling might somehow be the key to boxing. Hoping Jeffie
wouldn't be unnerved as he had been the last time, I smiled at
him, and I believe that I can say with some confidence that he
was not unnerved. What I thought I was doing was appealing
to his sense of humour, disarming him by inviting him to take
the whole thing about as seriously as I was taking it. What I

was in fact doing was provoking him, for he came at me harder than ever.

I smiled throughout the whole second round, so incensing my opponent, his supporters, and even a few of my supporters, that, by the end, more than half the people in the hall were cheering for Jeffie, exhorting him to wipe what they persisted in calling the "smug" smile off my face. Despite the fact that I obviously could not box, despite the fact that from the first bell to the last, I had done nothing but absorb punishment, they would not let go of the notion that at long last one of Father Seymour's Number was being whipped.

For years, as Uncle Reginald said later, it would be talked of as an upset, the night that Little Jeffie White beat one of Father Seymour's Number, one of the Divine Ryans, all over the ring. I was surprised that I hadn't been knocked out by this time. Even that thought struck me as funny. As I felt myself smiling again I wondered if I should go down, pretend to be knocked out. I made up my mind to do it, in fact tried to do it, but nothing happened. I smiled again at the thought that, with my luck, the only part of my brain that was damaged was the part that told my body how to fall.

The referee seemed to take my smile as a sign that I was not hurt and wanted to keep going, for he kept crouching down as if to see if I was still smiling. The strange thing was that, when I saw him looking at me, I couldn't help smiling at him even more. For one thing, I was sort of embarrassed by all the attention he was paying me, running around, looking at me—I had never been so closely scrutinized before, under any circumstances. I kept wondering what it was he was staring at, what it was I was doing wrong, and each time I caught his eye I smiled foolishly, not knowing what else to do. Also however, he began to strike me as being very funny, that is, not him per se, but the whole idea of the referee struck me as being funny, the referee whose job was not to keep one nine-year-old from beating up another, but to make sure that he did it properly, according to the rules, as well as to make sure that I submitted to it properly, according to the rules. It tickled me that he watched approvingly when we stood apart, punching one another, but intervened when we stopped fighting, when I threw my arms around the other boy and tried to rest. "Break," he said angrily, as if I was taking advantage of the other boy, as if it was unreasonable of me to deprive him of the chance of hitting me again.

Finally, the bell rang to end the second round. Everything was spinning and I had no idea where my corner was. "If yer dyin', see Reg Ryan," a voice said. Then I felt myself sitting down and the spinning stopped. "How do you feel, Draper Doyle?" said Uncle Reginald. All I could do was shake my head.

"Maybe we should stop the fight, Seymour," said Uncle Reginald. Father Seymour said nothing.

"Well what about it?" said Uncle Reginald.

"The boy isn't hurt," said Father Seymour, who obviously hoped that I would go the distance. I think Uncle Reginald would have stopped it, if it had been up to him, but it was not. As he said later, he could have thrown in a thousand towels and they would have been ignored.

In the third round, simply unable to take further punishment, I decided to try what the Protestant boy had tried with Young Leonard. When the bell rang, I came out of my corner with what to the audience must have seemed like more enthusiasm than was appropriate for a boxer who had been absorbing punishment for the last two rounds. We touched gloves and, as the other boy was about to back away, I got down on my hands and knees and grabbed him by the leg. It seemed to me that compared to him hitting me in the face, me grabbing him by the leg was no big deal, but the whole hall rang with booing.

All he wanted to do was break my nose, and here was I, clinging unreasonably to his leg.

"Booooo," the crowd roared.

"Stand up, Draper Doyle," screamed Father Seymour, sounding as if his worst fears had been realized. "Stand up and fight!"

The referee grabbed hold of me, dragged me to my feet, and to my surprise declared that the fight was not yet over. Perhaps he had grown so tired of seeing Father Seymour's boys beat up the Protestants, he didn't want to miss even one second of our comeuppance.

"Box," he said.

I was still looking at the referee when the other boy obeyed his command by throwing a roundhouse right that landed squarely on my jaw. Even as the ring was going round and the floor was coming up to meet me, it occurred to me that many more such encounters waited for me in the future. "If yer dyin', see Reg Ryan," said a voice inside my head. During that long fall to the floor, I thought of Mary and my mother, and of my father, whose ghost, even after six months of oralysis, was still appearing to me. What did my father want? I wondered. What on earth did my father want? It might have been from the sheer effort of trying to answer this question, from sheer confusion that my head was spinning. Then I blacked out.

"Draper Doyle," I heard a voice saying. "Draper Doyle." It was Uncle Reginald, kneeling over me. "Draper Doyle," he said, "are you all right?"

I smiled at him.

In the dressing room afterwards, Father Seymour maintained a kind of contemptuous silence on the subject of my behaviour. He had to, what with Uncle Reginald being there, looking at him as if he was daring him to say something. While Uncle Reginald attended to my cuts and bruises, Father Seymour went about tousling the hair of the other boys whose faces, almost without exception, were unmarked. The other boys were silent until Uncle Reginald said that instead of showering I should go straight home. As he led me out of the dressing room, a few of them said "so long" in a way that seemed meant to be pointedly sympathetic. There was a party planned for all the boys, Father Seymour said, but Uncle Reginald, shouting over his shoulder, assured him that I was in no condition to attend it.

When we were in the car, I asked him what he thought of my performance. Actually, Uncle Reginald said, I hadn't done too badly. The other boy had been swinging wildly throughout the fight, and it was only my unfailing ability to put my head exactly in the path of his fists that had made him look so good.

"Such head speed," Uncle Reginald said, "such timing!"

Perhaps, he said, if I had worn my goalie equipment, especially my mask, I might have had a chance. He could have beaten me up all day if I had those on. I could just see it. In this corner, a goalie. At least I wouldn't have black eyes.

"I guess you didn't win," Mary said, when we got home. Uncle Reginald had me in his arms. I was half knocked out. There was blood all over me. I guess you didn't win.

"Of course I won," I said. "All this happened on the way home."

Laughing, Uncle Reginald said, "No, he did not win. There is still no known instance of a boxer making a comeback while lying unconscious on the canvas." That was a good one. Still, I had to get back at Mary. It may have had something to do with my semi-conscious state that the following couplet appeared fully formed in my head: "Mary's tits are hard to find, they're not as big as her behind." Aunt Phil was there, but it didn't matter. You can get away with almost anything when you're half knocked out.

"Oh my God," my mother said when she saw me. She put her hand over her mouth and looked on the verge of tears until, as if she had suddenly realized that having your mother look at you in horror could, to say the least, be disconcerting, she managed a smile, then had Uncle Reginald carry me to bed, where in a few seconds I fell asleep.

The next day, my mother withheld comment, in fact ignored Father Seymour when he assured her that I was not hurt as badly as I appeared to be. It was obvious that although she knew that something had to be done about Father Seymour, she was not yet sure what that something was.

Within a couple of days, she was teasing me about my fight. She laughed when Mary called me Raccoon Face. The day after that, she called me Purple Puss. Every day, for about two weeks, my face changed colour, and every day Mary and my mother had a new name for me.

"Is it a bird?" Mary said. "Is it a plane? No, it's Kaleidohead."

"I wonder what colour Draper Doyle will be tomorrow," my mother would say, each night at the dinner table. They looked at me, Mary and my mother, examined me, two experts in facial coloration, consulting, comparing notes. Prognosis? "Green," Mary might say, "with bluish tints around the eyes." My mother would concur.

It was very distressing, going to bed not knowing what colour you would be when you got up. They should make a movie, Mary said, a short sequence of time-lapse photography called *The Changing Face of Draper Doyle*.

✦

My face was all but back to normal by the time Confession Wednesday came around. I spent the hours leading up to my confession rehearsing what I would say. I kept remembering

Young Leonard's face as Father Seymour led him from the ring. I had lost my fight, but Father Seymour could still have his moral victory if I confessed to cheating. I repeatedly imagined myself saying the words "I cheated at the boxing tournament." I said them over and over in my mind, trying to convince myself that to say them out loud would be just as easy.

In the confessional that afternoon, I recited the standard sin-ventory, listing six infractions of the junior ten commandments.

"Anything else?" Father Seymour said.

"No," I surprised myself by saying. "No, nothing else."

"Are you sure?" he said, hanging on "sure" as if he had been about to say my name.

I had a moment of panic, wondering what I would do if he withheld his forgiveness. I tried to remember if anyone else had been waiting for confession. If I was the last one, he could keep me in there until I told him what he wanted.

"Are you sure that's all?" he said.

"I'm sure," I said.

There might as well have been no screen between us, no darkness. All that was keeping us apart, all that was keeping the sacrament intact, was his unwillingness to say my name. Finally, I heard him sigh, and as his hand came up to give me absolution, I bowed my head.

"Go in peace," my uncle said. "Your sins have been forgiven."

13

HOPING TO encourage Uncle Reginald to devote further sessions to hockey, I took the puck my father had given me when I was seven to oralysis. As it turned out, Uncle Reginald had never seen the puck before. He read aloud from the piece of paper that was taped to one side of it: "Deflected into the stands by Canadiens goalie Gerry MacNeil at 1:03 of overtime. Caught by Donald Ryan. Nineteen seconds later, Elmer Lach scored to win the Stanley Cup for Montreal. Montreal Forum, April 16, 1953."

Uncle Reginald stood up and, turning the puck over and over in his hands much as my father had done at the Christmas concert, he shook his head and smiled.

"Well I'll be," he said. "So Donny was at that game."

"You remember it," I said.

"I do," he said, "I do, indeed. I listened to it on the radio." His voice was trembling.

"Is something wrong, Uncle Reginald?" I said.

"You've never heard of your father's missing year, have you?" he said, handing the puck back to me. When I shook my head, he sat down.

"Of course you haven't," he said. "Even your mother hasn't heard of it. It's something of a family secret."

He went on to tell me that after his graduation from Oxford, my father had failed to come home as planned. The whole family had gone to meet him at the airport, only to find that he was not on the plane. His father contacted Oxford, but they had no idea of his whereabouts. He then notified the police in London, who soon discovered that instead of taking the plane to St. John's, my father had taken one to Montreal. Reg Ryan Sr.'s first thought was that his son had welshed on his side of their agreement and had gone to Montreal to join the priesthood. He contacted all the seminaries in Quebec, asking them if anyone by the name of Donald Ryan had applied for acceptance. When he was told that no one by that name had, he sent them a photograph of my father who might, he said, have used another name. Even when he was told that no one answering to the photograph had turned up at any of the seminaries, Reg Ryan Sr. was convinced that it was only a matter of time. He waited three months before finally contacting the police in Montreal who, because my father had obviously gone there of his own accord, refused to conduct anything more than a short check of phone directories and rental listings. No one by the name of Donald Ryan turned up, and that, as far as they were concerned, was the end of it.

At home, opinion was unanimous that disappearing was more like something Uncle Reginald would do. They all kept saying that the last person they would have thought capable of doing such a thing was Donald Ryan. The family used the word "missing" to describe his situation, though "hiding," as Uncle Reginald often pointed out, would have been more like it. They did not let on to anyone that he was "missing." He was in Montreal, they told the many people who had heard that he was coming home from Oxford. He had stopped off in St. John's, but only for a few days, not long enough to see anyone but his own family. He was going to "work" in Montreal for "a while" and then come home.

Still, before long, there were rumours, which Reg Ryan Sr. blamed on Uncle Reginald, who in fact was not to blame for them. Donald Ryan had run off, people said. Donald Ryan was hiding from his family. Donald Ryan was involved in some sort of business dealings in Montreal of which his family, if they found out about them, would not approve. At the height of the rumours, Reg Ryan Sr. hired a private investigator, but after a month of searching, the man turned up nothing.

It was just over a year after he failed to show up at the airport, when his family had all but given up on him and were telling one another that they would never see him again, that they received a letter from him, a letter which made no mention whatsoever of the missing year, containing nothing but a terse request for airfare from Montreal to St. John's. A few days later he was home, back in his father's house where, despite all the shouting that was done, not just by his parents but by his brothers and sisters as well, all of them demanding that he explain himself, he refused to say one word about his year in Montreal. Nor did he ever say anything about it. In fact, Uncle Reginald said, in surprisingly little time the family stopped mentioning the matter and my father slipped quite easily into the life which, for one whole year, had been waiting for him.

He had been in Montreal from May 1952 to May 1953. In other words, it was during his missing year that he had gone to the Forum and caught the puck I now held in my hands.

Uncle Reginald took from the shelves which lined his apartment one of his many hockey books, in which he said there was a photograph taken that same night at the Forum. He opened the book out on the floor and, getting down on our hands and knees, we looked at the photograph. At first we were very excited, for the photograph was of the part of the Forum where my father would most likely have been sitting. It was taken just after the goal was scored in overtime. It showed, not the Boston zone, where Elmer Lach was no doubt being mobbed by his team-mates, but the Montreal zone, where

Gerry MacNeil, still standing all alone in the net, was in the process of throwing his goalie stick and glove up in the air. My father, to have caught a puck from MacNeil's stick, must have been sitting somewhere in the area which formed the background to the photograph, either behind or to the right or the left of the Montreal net.

We tried to find him in that sea of upraised arms, going over the photograph inch by inch, Uncle Reginald even using his OED magnifying glass. However, most of the faces, caught in the act of celebrating victory, were either badly blurred or obscured by people waving hats and scarves. None of those few faces in the background which were clearly photographed belonged to him. Somewhere among the hats and overcoats, among the black and white of 1953, my father, if the inscription on the puck was true, was standing with the others, holding the puck which I now held in my hands. Nineteen and some seconds before the photograph was taken, at 1:03 of overtime, the puck had come flying from the ice towards him. I turned the puck over. On the other side, in block numerals cut from paper, it read 1:03. Moment 1:03 had come falling from the sky and he had caught it, saved it. But the rest of that year in Montreal was still missing, perhaps even gone forever.

Later that night, I stood at my bedroom window, watching the house across the way, wondering what my father had done with his missing year, why he had gone from Oxford to Montreal. I knew that he had attended Oxford on a Rhodes Scholarship. Among those qualifications needed to become a Rhodes Scholar was proficiency in at least one sport. My father's sport was hockey, which he had played with average ability in high school. Not that he was the classic scholar/athlete by any means. There was the problem of his size for instance. The rumour the year that he applied was that there were unofficial height and weight requirements, it being the opinion of the selection committee that a Rhodes scholar should stand no less than five foot eight and weigh at least one hundred fifty pounds. My father, who fell considerably short of both these marks, wrote five-eight, one-hundred-fifty on his application form, and, according to Uncle Reginald, went to his interview in mortal fear of being weighed and measured. It turned out, however, that, while my father was not the sort of manly scholar they were said to be looking for, he won the scholarship anyway. Uncle Reginald always suspected that unknown to my father, Reg Ryan Sr. had pulled some strings for him.

About what my father had done at Oxford aside from study scholastic philosophy, I knew next to nothing. He claimed to have played centre for a hockey team made up exclusively of Rhodes scholars. "The Rhodes Blades" they were called. Most of them were Canadians, a few were Americans, and one, their captain, said to have been named Lord Rumsey and related to the Queen, was from Great Britain. The Rhodes Blades, my father said, disbanded undefeated in 1952. Against which teams had they compiled their undefeated record? According to my father, against the Olympic teams of certain little-known European countries who came to Oxford to challenge them. He said the closest they had come to losing was their victory in over-time against the Estonian Ice Hockey Federation, for whom "the legendary Kron Vladsky" was playing goal.

Needless to say, I took the very existence of the Rhodes Blades with a grain of salt, suspecting the whole thing to have been an elaborate joke, perhaps cooked up by the so-called Lord Rumsey for whom ice hockey must have been one of those New World oddities that cried out to be lampooned.

It seemed not unlikely that the Rhodes Blades had been together for only as long as it took to have their picture taken. There was a photograph of them, the only photograph from my father's time at Oxford, in my album.

I took the album from the closet and found at the very front the photo of the Rhodes Blades, taken at Oxford in 1950. They were posing in a kind of turn-of-the-century, back-at-the-club manner, a group of gentleman hockey players, lounging about in armchairs in front of the fire, their sticks, emblems of their sport, scattered about, the Rhodes Blades suffering themselves to be photographed, allowing the world a rare glimpse into their private lives. The only thing wrong with this back-at-the-club photograph was that, though the Rhodes Blades were wearing blazers and slacks and sitting cross-legged in their armchairs, they were also, all of them, wearing skates. Even the man who was standing by the fireplace, holding a snifter of brandy in one hand and a pipe in the other, was absurdly elevated on a pair of skates. Lord Rumsey, cigar in hand, legs elegantly crossed, was quite nonchalantly wearing skates. My father, sitting across from him, was wearing skates which, for the way that he was looking at the camera, might have been club slippers. They were all affecting the kind of insolence normal to such photographs, but also smirking slightly, not so much, it seemed to me, to acknowledge the obvious joke as to suggest that there was some further, private joke involved, some joke behind the joke, some riddle that they were daring you to solve.

After leaving Oxford, after leaving the Rhodes Blades, my father had failed to rejoin the Divine Ryans, the team for which, in my mind, at least, he had played centre. The Divine Ryans. I imagined them on bubblegum cards. Aunt Phil on right wing. Uncle Reginald on left wing. Father Francis and Father Seymour on defence. Sister Louise between the pipes. Their pictures on one side, their lifetime stats on the other. Instead of goals and assists, masses and confessions. I could see it now. "Reg Ryan Jr. has been in a terrible slump since 1952." These, on the other hand, might have been Aunt Phil's stats for

1967: M 156, C 52, TP 208. "Philomena Ryan, known to her team-mates as Aunt Phil, has led the League in scoring for thirteen of the past twenty-five years." All they lacked was a centreman. All they lacked, as in 1952 – 53, was my father, without whom they would be playing shorthanded from now on.

I went back to the window. Across the way in the backyard, on a small, spotlit patch of ice, my father stood, looking as though he had skated out of the darkness just in time to have his picture taken. Dressed in a numberless Habs uniform, he was smiling as though to a nation that adored him, as though this very picture would soon be on bubblegum cards throughout the country. Easing forward on his skates, he crouched over as if to take a faceoff, his stick in front of him. Then, as if there had been some delay and he must make his approach again, he coasted in a circle, turning his back to me, then coming round, head down, easing forward, as if some invisible linesman was about to drop the puck. He kept on repeating this manoeuvre, over and over, coasting slowly in a circle, then coming back, head down, for the face off, then turning away. I opened the window and was about to call out to him when he looked up at me the way a player might look at a linesman who was taking too long to drop the puck. The puck he had given me, the one memento from his missing year, was still in my hand. I held it between thumb and forefinger, held it up so he could see it, and he nodded. Then he coasted in a circle and, as he came forward for the faceoff, I threw the puck, threw it underhand, as far and as high as I could.

I watched it go up end over end, spinning, revolving so rapidly that it no longer looked like a puck but more like a piece of black and white glass glittering beneath the streetlamp. It went so high that for a few moments it disappeared into the darkness overhead. And then it reappeared, fluttering down, end over end, minus the paper which seemed to have simply

vanished. A plain black puck it was now, barely visible against
the darkness, spinning, until at the last second it straightened
out and landed on my side of the fence, leaving only the faintest,
slot-shaped indentation in the snow.

When I looked up to see what my father had made of my
hopelessly inadequate toss, there was no sign of him. Even the
spotlit patch of ice was gone. I ran downstairs and, putting on
my coat and boots, and taking a flashlight from the porch, went
outdoors. I found the place in the snow, the slot through which
the puck had disappeared, and reached down with my hand,
groping all the way to the ground without success. I put the
flashlight down and began digging in the snow with both hands,
sifting through it. Among that soft whiteness, one hard, black
puck should not have been difficult to find, and yet I couldn't
find it. It seemed to have gone, not only through the snow, but
through the ground, to have been swallowed up, to have disappeared as completely as the piece of paper which had been
attached to it.

I lay on my back in the snow, looking up as if the puck that
had come falling from the sky was not my puck, as if the puck
from my father's missing year might still come down.

14

"WOULD YOU do us the honour of taking us to St. Martin's Cemetery, Father Seymour?" Aunt Phil said. It conjured up an image of Father Seymour walking arm-in-arm between her and my mother, a widow on either side, leading them, with an air of grim chivalry, to their husbands' graves, while the rest of the family walked behind him. It was the anniversary of my father's death (and also of his birth, though this fact went unmentioned). Father Seymour consented to take us to the graveyard, though our procession was nothing like I imagined it, for Father Seymour could hardly have walked arm-in-arm between two widows who were taller than he was. What Father Seymour taking us to St. Martin's in fact consisted of was Aunt Phil walking well in front of the rest of us, then Father Seymour, keeping just far enough ahead of my mother going up the hill that, while he seemed to be walking with her, he did not have to speak to her. Then came Mary and me, far behind, pushing Sister Louise, each of us holding one handle of the wheelchair.

It was late March, but almost all the snow was gone. Though Fleming Street still had that grey, late-winter look about it, the weather was warm enough that we could shed the overcoats and boots we had been wearing since last December.

When Aunt Phil reached the gates of the cemetery, she turned around, looking down at us as she might have looked down from heaven at five souls still struggling to make it. By the time the rest of us got there, she was strolling through the graveyard, pointing out the headstones of people who had been waked at Reg Ryan's. "There's one of ours," she was saying. She stopped to tidy up the grave, removing last fall's dead leaves from the base of the headstone. No one had ever been able to convince Aunt Phil that our obligation to our customers ended with the funeral, that we did not have to tend their graves for all eternity.

We followed her to her husband's headstone, to "His" headstone, rather, beside which was a stone bearing her name and date of birth, with the date of death still to be inscribed. We knelt on the concrete border of the grave while Father Seymour and Sister Louise led us in a prayer, and then we stood again.

"He's free now," Aunt Phil said, brushing the dust from her knees. "Free from the marriage bed."

"Oh for God's sake," my mother said, looking around as if there must be someone in the graveyard who shared her exasperation at this remark.

Aunt Phil turned to face her, but before she could say anything, Sister Louise intervened. "Remember where you are," she said severely, looking at my mother and then at Aunt Phil. "Remember what day this is."

Both of them stared at the ground, and it seemed for a moment that that would be the end of it. Father Seymour headed off towards my father's grave, and we all began to follow him—all of us, that is, except my mother, who hung back, her arms at her sides; her purse, which she held by one hand, hung almost to the ground.

"I'm not going," she said. The words came out with a great exhalation of breath, as if she was simply too weary to make the visit. "I'm not going, not today."

"I want you to stop this nonsense, Linda," Sister Louise said. "The children—"

"I'm not going," my mother said, her eyes blinking back a sudden rush of tears. Then, as if she must say it so quickly that none of them could interrupt, she blurted out "Mine was free from the marriage bed before he died."

She turned and, all but trailing her purse on the ground, walked to the cemetery gates. There she stopped, but only to reach down and remove her high-heeled shoes, which she stuffed in her purse. She did it so matter-of-factly, it might have been no more than what one normally did when leaving a cemetery. Then she began to run.

Despite Aunt Phil, who tried to stop us, Mary and I hurried to the graveyard fence the better to see our mother. The Young Widow, her black dress hiked above her knees, was all but sprinting down Fleming Street, wearing nothing on her feet but nylons, her purse trailing behind her as though she might use it to fend off anyone who tried to stop her. What the people of Fleming Street must have thought upon seeing that long-legged apparition running barefoot down the hill, I still cannot imagine.

The rest of us went to my father's grave without her, Aunt Phil, Sister Louise, and Father Seymour all having tacitly agreed to ignore what had happened. Afterwards, once we had seen Sister Louise back to the convent, we headed home. Judging by the number of curtains we saw moving, it was noted by every household on Fleming Street that despite the Young Widow's example, the rest of the Divine Ryans walked home, still wearing shoes.

At dinner that night, Aunt Phil said nothing to our mother, though she was quite impressive non-verbally, slamming down each plate just short of breaking it. After dinner, Uncle Reginald came downstairs, and when I had him alone for a moment, I told him what had happened, told him of how my mother had run down Fleming Street, with her dress hiked up above her knees and her black purse trailing pennant-like behind her. He smiled and nodded his head as if he had long been expecting that very thing to happen.

Later, Sister Louise and Father Seymour came over, it being only right, Aunt Phil said pointedly, that a man's family gather on the anniversary of his death. Still, not one word was said about what had happened. In fact, nothing much was said at all, until my mother spoke up.

"I think," she said, "I'd like to stop working at Reg Ryan's and go back to school."

Aunt Phil, Father Seymour, and Sister Louise, though they were soon voicing their opposition to this idea, seemed a little relieved, looking at one another as if to say "So that's what it was all about."

"You've no need to go back to school, Linda," Aunt Phil said, almost reassuringly, as if our mother did not so much want to go back as think she had to. "You and the children will be well looked after."

"Of course," said Sister Louise, taking Aunt Phil's tone, "Of course you will. It's only natural that on a day like this you'd start to worry about such things." There was much nodding of heads. It seemed my mother's run down Fleming Street had been explained away without anyone having had to say one word about it.

My mother sat there for a while, saying nothing, looking now and then at Uncle Reginald who kept smiling at her. Then she spoke up again. "It's not just the children," she said. "I'd just like to go back to school, that's all, do something else besides help run a funeral home."

"Reg Ryan's," Aunt Phil said, "has been good enough for everyone else who ever married into this family."

"I'd just like to get an education," my mother said.

"Of course you would," said Uncle Reginald.

"Now don't you start," Aunt Phil said, pointing at him, "don't you start."

"Why shouldn't a young woman like Linda have an education?" said Uncle Reginald.

"More people have ruined their minds by getting an education," Aunt Phil said, "than have gone to hell, and that's saying something."

"Donald had an education," said Uncle Reginald.

For a while, there was silence. Then Aunt Phil turned to Sister Louise. "To think," she said, almost tearfully, her voice breaking, "to think that this man has his father's name."

"I'd rather have his money," said Uncle Reginald, at which Aunt Phil stood up and pointed at him.

"You'll burn," she said, "you'll burn," as if he had already burned, as if there was nothing on the chair across from her but a pile of ashes. Soon after, with Father Seymour and Sister Louise doing their best to keep Aunt Phil and Uncle Reginald apart, the gathering broke up.

✦

One night, later that week, I woke to the sound of someone whispering my name. "Draper Doyle." My first thought was a visitation—after so often appearing to me from a distance, my father had finally made up his mind to come closer and to talk to me. Sitting up in bed, however, I saw, looking at me through the barely opened door, not my father but my mother.

"Draper Doyle," she said again.

"What?" I said.

She motioned with her hand. "Come on," she said, "we're going to my room."

When I got out of bed, I saw Mary standing behind her. Mary put her finger to her lips, then began to tiptoe down the hall in a kind of parody of stealth, lifting her feet much higher than she had to, crouching over like one of those absurdly devious cartoon villains. I started to laugh but my mother put her hand over my mouth and kept it there until all three of us were in her room and the door was closed.

"What are we doing?" I whispered. Instead of answering, the two of them sat crosslegged on the bed. The room was so dark I could hardly see them.

"Draper Doyle," my mother said, in a kind of mock French accent.

"What?" I said.

"Would you lak to join zee Reseestance?" It was hard to believe that this was my mother speaking.

"The what?" I said.

"Zee Reseestance," she said. "Eeet wahl be danjerous but vary exciting, mon ami."

Finally, abandoning the accent, my mother told me what was going on. She said that she and Mary had been "meeting" every night for a week, and had decided that it was time to "bring me in."

"So," she said, "would you lak to join zee Reseestance?"

I said I would, though I still had no idea what it was.

It turned out that the "Resistance" had been Uncle Reginald's idea. In fact, it was really group oralysis, without the oralyst.

That first night, we talked about something that, as it turned out, had occurred to each of us at one time or another. Why was it, Mary was the first to wonder out loud, that, despite her size, Aunt Phil was able to walk so much faster than the rest of us? It seemed it would remain a mystery until our mother ventured the theory that Aunt Phil had achieved such perfect equilibrium between her bosom and her backside that their net effect on her was zero. There followed a kind of silent fit of giggles, a furtive snorting which might have convinced anyone listening from outside that, our lives depending on it, the three of us were trying to keep a cow from mooing.

The Resistance began meeting almost every night after that. Our ultimate mission, our mother said, was to locate and destroy the enemy's "dehumourizer," a little-known household appliance. After we swore an oath to the accomplishment of this task, she explained that according to Uncle Reginald Aunt Phil had had something called a dehumourizer installed in the house twenty years ago. "Does anyone else find it funny in here?" she'd say, then go to turn on the dehumourizer, the location of which only she knew. The dehumourizer, Uncle Reginald said, might even be disguised as something else, a toaster, a dishwasher. One thing was certain, it seemed to me. She had had it on full blast since we moved in.

One night, the subject of our group oralysis session was my boxing match. If a Catholic had had to fight a Protestant, my mother said, why had they not sent Aunt Phil up against Millie Barter? We'd have been sure to win, given that Aunt Phil outweighed Millie by at least a hundred pounds. We tried to imagine it. "In the blue corner, weighing eighty pounds, that mesmerizing Protestant from down the street, Millie 'The Mosquito' Barter. Barter. And in the red corner, weighing one hundred eighty pounds, the Mighty Mick herself, the Bruising Floozy From St. John's, the one, the only, Philomena. Mena." I tried, without much success, to imagine Aunt Phil in boxing shorts and boxing gloves. I fared better with Millie Barter, imagined her shaking her whole body to keep loose before the fight, her aged white head bobbing back and forth, her frail liver-spotted little arms performing a mesmerizing series of uppercuts.

After rolling in giggles on the bed for a while, the three of us sat up against the headboard, my mother in the middle.

"Mom," Mary said, "are you going to get married again?"

My mother made a face and shrugged.

"Is it because of us?" Mary said. "Is it because no man would want to marry a woman with two children?"

"Where did you hear that?" my mother said.

"Aunt Phil," Mary said. "She said you don't want to get married anyway, but even if you did, it wouldn't matter, because of us."

Shaking her head, my mother said something under her breath, then put her arms around us, hugging us tightly to her. She looked back and forth between us. "Who wouldn't want to marry us?" she said. "They'd have to be crazy. Why, just the other day, I put an ad in the paper. Young Widow adept at running funeral home, nine-year-old boxing goalie, and twelve-year-old prone to wearing bras outside her clothes seek arrangement with sensible young man—"

"But Mom—" Mary said.

"But Mom nothing," my mother said. "You worry about your own love life. From what Draper Doyle told me, it could use some worry."

"I never told her anything," I said, before Mary could accuse me.

"You did so," my mother said, "you told me Mary is madly in love with a boy named Sir Egbert Hippiehead, a.k.a. Harold Noonan."

Mary groaned and, pulling away from my mother, covered her head with a pillow.

"I hate Draper Doyle," she said. "I will never speak to him again."

"Yes," my mother said. "Sir Egbert Hippiehead. If you don't want him, maybe I'll marry him. Maybe I'll write him a letter. 'Dear Hippiehead, how I long to run my fingers through your hair.'"

Mary gave a muffled groan from beneath the pillow. "Yeccchhh," she said. "I wouldn't kiss him if God told me to."

It wasn't long before these night-time meetings began to affect how we carried on throughout the day. It got so that if the three of us were even in the same room, we started laughing. We could let nothing go by without remarking on it. Mealtimes were especially bad. With Aunt Phil, the subject of a good many of our secret jokes, sitting there among us, we couldn't help ourselves. Just looking at one another set us off.

At first Aunt Phil made nothing of our strange behaviour. She seemed to think that if ignored it might go away. One night, however, when we had cow's tongue for dinner, we got to her. I kept mooing all through dinner. I put mustard on the tongue. "You hate mustard," Mary said. "Yes," I said, "but the cow likes it." Among the questions arising from this remark were: 1) Could a cow's tongue taste the people who were eating it? 2) Could the people who were eating it tell what the cow's last meal had been? "I swear," Aunt Phil said, getting up from the table and looking at my mother, "that you and your children are going crazy."

One night, later that week, when I was wakened by voices, I thought it was Mary and my mother come to get me again. But then I realized that the voices were coming from Aunt Phil's room. I got out of bed as quietly as I could and tiptoed down the hall, putting my ear to Aunt Phil's door.

"There is no need for such theatrics," Aunt Phil was saying.

"No," my mother said, "I suppose not."

"Frankly," Aunt Phil said, "I'd have thought that I deserved better treatment."

For a while, there was silence, and then I heard what I took to be my mother sitting down on Aunt Phil's bed.

"Aunt Phil," she said, "I think it would be best for everyone if the children and I moved out."

"Nonsense," Aunt Phil said. "We could never afford it."

"I'm not asking you to afford it," my mother said.

"What do you mean?"

"Well. We wouldn't just be moving out. We'd move away. We'd—"

"Away?" Aunt Phil said. "What do you mean by away? Away from Fleming Street?"

"Well, yes," my mother said, "but further than that. To some place where jobs are easier to come by. I'll need a part-time job—"

"My dear, you're talking nonsense," Aunt Phil said. "What kind of life could you give the children? They're used to a much better life than you could give them, I assure you."

"I can get some sort of job," my mother said, "and go to university part-time if I have to. I've thought it out—"

"My dear, you can't have thought it out. You can't have. Here, in this city, on this street, you belong to one of the better families. Anywhere else, you simply wouldn't belong."

"Aunt Phil, I'm sorry to have to say this, but I'm not asking for your approval. Now I'm grateful for everything you've done for us, I really am, but we're moving out."

"Well," Aunt Phil said. "I'm just as sorry to have to say that I can't let you."

My mother laughed. "Can't let us? What do you mean you can't let us?"

"Exactly that," Aunt Phil said. "If you feel you have to go, I won't try to stop you. But I cannot let you take Donald's children."

"Donald's children?" my mother said. "Donald is dead, Aunt Phil. They're my children. And besides, how do you propose to stop me from taking them?"

"You're a single woman," Aunt Phil said. "You've no education, no job to go to, no prospects."

"So?" my mother said, "I'm not saying we'd have an easy time of it—"

"So," Aunt Phil said. "So. Since you make me say it, here it is. We wouldn't need to add much to that list of shortcomings to convince a court that you're unsuitable."

My mother said nothing.

"We wouldn't want to do it, of course. But we would do it if it meant the future of this family."

"What are you talking about?"

"I'm sure I don't have to say it straight out," Aunt Phil said. "Now you know what I mean. Who do you think the courts would listen to, if it came to that?"

"I can't believe what you're saying—"

"My dear, if you can't, then you must have been born yesterday. Now none of this need happen. None of it will happen as long as you give up this foolish idea."

"You're telling me," my mother said, "that you would make up some story about me, take my children from me?"

"My dear, it's time that you grew up. You can't have thought that we would just let you walk away with the children. Now if you feel you have to leave, I won't stop you, but the children stay with us."

"That's what you want, isn't it?" my mother said. "Now that I've said what I've said, you want me to leave. Go off by myself. That would be very convenient, wouldn't it?"

"Don't be absurd," Aunt Phil said. "You're still a part of this family. If you want to be."

"My God," my mother said. "You don't expect us to go on as usual after this, do you?"

"I would have no trouble doing so," Aunt Phil said. "You will have to make up your own mind about it. Now please go back to bed. Tomorrow is a day like any other."

With that I heard footsteps coming towards the door and

just managed to duck into the bathroom across the hall before my mother came out, crying, her two hands over her mouth. I watched through the crack in the door as she went down the hall to her room. Then I tiptoed back to mine and got in bed.

15

O UR GROUP sessions ended quite abruptly, my mother refusing to explain when Mary asked her why. Not letting on that I had overheard the conversation, I too asked my mother what was wrong, but she said "Nothing," and for a while gave every sign of lapsing back to her old self. My Momary dreams, though they were not more horrifying than usual, become more frequent, so that I soon found myself buying two pairs of underwear a week, and I had to ask—" to forgo my oralysis fee. Surprisingly, he did so without asking for an explanation.

One day, I went to Woolworth's to get a replacement for the pair of underwear I had soiled the day before. For some reason, after having over the past few months sold me at least twenty pairs of underwear without saying a word, the sales clerk finally spoke up.

"May I ask," she said, "what you do with all the underwear?"

I felt myself blushing and looked at the floor.

"Is all the underwear for you?" she said, smiling at me.

She was probably just having fun with me. I should have said "Yes, of course it is. What kind of nine-year-old would buy underwear for someone else?" Or I should have said "It's none of your business." But no, I had to panic, had to open my big mouth.

"I'm from St. Martin's Orphanage," I said. "I'm in Father Seymour's Number. He sends me here to buy underwear for all the boys."

She raised her eyebrows. "He has you buy them one pair at a time?" she said. "One pair per week?"

"Yes Ma'am," I said.

"How many boys are at the orphanage?" she said.

"About two hundred," I said.

"And they all wear the same size underwear? Size small?"

"Well, I'm in charge of buying the small sizes," I said. "Another boy buys medium, and another boy buys large."

"Well, they don't buy them here," she said. "You're the only boy I know who has bought twenty pairs of underwear this year. Of any size."

"Well," I said, "I guess they buy them somewhere else."

"I guess they do," she said. Now she was looking at me with what might have been suspicion.

"What's your name?" she said. Panic again. Why couldn't I have said Joe Blow or John Smith? But no, I could do better than that. The first name that came to mind that I was fairly certain she would not have heard of was that of Eric Nesterenko, who played right wing for the Chicago Black Hawks.

"Eric Nesterenko," I said.

She raised her eyebrows. "Is that really your name?" she said. When I nodded, she picked up a pencil.

"How do you spell it?" she said. I spelled it.

"OK, Eric," she said, handing me my (world-record-setting?) twenty-first pair of underwear. "See you next week."

"Bye," I said, vowing never to return.

How could I have known that the next day Father Seymour would call the entire orphanage to assembly in the dining hall?

"Today, we have a new boy joining us," he said. It was standard practice to call assembly when a new boy joined the orphanage—the only problem was that the new boy was usually at Father Seymour's side when he was introduced, but this time there was no one.

"Our new boy," said Father Seymour, "is standing among you at this very moment." Everyone looked around, stood on tiptoe, searching for the new boy.

"I want you to raise him on your shoulders when you find him," Father Seymour said. For five minutes, there was mass confusion, everyone searching for the apparently non-existent new boy. We all looked at Father Seymour.

"There's no new boy, Father," someone said, and everyone laughed.

"Oh indeed there is," said Father Seymour. "Indeed there is. His name is Eric Nesterenko."

Great guffaws of laughter went up.

The only possible explanation was that the sales clerk had phoned Father Seymour, who must have gathered, from her description of the clothes that I was wearing—the Habs insignia was everywhere—that I was Nesterenko.

"Eric Nesterenko?" Young Leonard said. "He plays for the Black Hawks, Father."

"Indeed he does," said Father Seymour, who, I suspected, had not known that Eric Nesterenko was a hockey player, let alone what team he played for, until one of the Brothers told him. "But it seems that a boy by the same name also buys underwear at Woolworth's."

"Are you feeling all right, Father?" someone said, to much snickering.

"Feeling fine," said Father Seymour, then looked directly at me. "Yes," he said, "it seems Eric Nesterenko buys underwear for all of you. Or some of you at least, those of you who wear size small."

There was a mystified silence in the hall.

"It seems," said Father Seymour, "that a boy claiming to be Nesterenko and to be in charge of buying small underwear for St. Martin's Orphanage has bought over twenty pairs of Stanfield's whites since last fall."

The other boys should have been able to tell that I was Nesterenko from the mere fact that I was the only one in the whole hall not laughing.

"I wonder," Father Seymour said, "if Mr. Eric Nesterenko would be man enough to step forward. When he does, I want the boys of my Number to carry him about the hall on your shoulders."

They were all around me, the boys of Father Seymour's Number, ready to bear me in mock triumph on their shoulders, should I be so foolish as to reveal myself.

I turned and, crashing open the fire-escape door, all but fell down the steps, at the bottom of which I began to run. Before I had gotten halfway across the field, I was crying, bawling I would have said, if it had been someone else who was doing it. I could hear myself, breathing sulkily with every step, sniffling. I ran faster, fighting the wind, fleeing some sulking, bawling version of myself, scorning him and his filthy underwear and his having a bum to be ashamed of and his little, hairless, wrinkled Methuselah between his legs.

When I reached the other side of the field, when I was about halfway up the embankment off Fleming Street, I felt a hand wrench back my collar and I turned around to find myself caught, run down by Father Seymour who, all that time, must have been chasing me and was now looking at me as if to say that on top of everything else, I had tried to get away from him.

He took me in his arms toddler-fashion, one arm beneath my backside, the other around my waist, and all but ran with me towards the rectory. As he began to climb the stairs to his office, I began to struggle, my upper body twisting, undulating, so that he had to adjust his grip to get better hold of me. Then, so suddenly that he almost dropped me, I went limp. Once again, Father Seymour changed his grip, and once again I began to struggle. Back and forth I went as we climbed the stairs, alternating between what might have been hysteria and abject resignation, with each transformation slipping further down in Father Seymour's arms, so that Father Seymour was now hugging me to his chest, now to his stomach, now to his crotch, now to his upper thighs, until soon, at the top of the stairs, he barely had hold of me.

At the top step he stumbled and went into a flurry of panicked back-pedalling which, while it kept us from falling down the stairs, also robbed him of his balance, so that after a doomed attempt to regain it by running even faster, he fell crashing to the floor. This somehow combined with a frantic hoisting of my body, so that when Father Seymour lay prone, I lay perfectly on top of him, my arms still flailing one minute, still going limp the next.

It was only at this moment that he acknowledged what was happening by letting out a loud sigh of relief. There we were, so neatly arranged on the floor that the whole thing might have been rehearsed. Even as he lay there, on his back with me belly-up on top of him, rising and falling on his chest each time he breathed, Father Seymour remained composed. It was almost as if, from the moment I had started struggling to the moment we fell to the floor, he had followed some recommended procedure, some officially approved method of losing your grip on a nine-year-old.

Finally, I stopped moving and raised my head to look through the perfect v formed by Father Seymour's shoes. "Get off me," he said, "get off me this instant," as if my whole purpose had been to pin him to the floor in just this manner. I did as he said, got off him and stood up. Looking somewhat embarrassed by the fact that I was on my feet while he was still climbing to his, he got up and began brushing the dust from his clothes. He looked over his shoulder, pulling his coat forward to see if there was any on his back, then turned around. "Did I miss any?" he said, looking at me as if to say that, first of all, he had not the slightest reason to feel foolish, and second that his enlisting my help in knocking the dust from his clothes did not mean that I was off the hook.

I shook my head to indicate that he had not missed any dust, though in fact he had. Then he was standing in front of me, red-faced and still fighting for breath. He took off his belt and I realized that I was about to have the Doyle drapered out of me. A photograph of me, tear-stained and bawling, reduced to repentant sulking, would be sent to Mary and Harold Noonan, not to mention Aunt Phil. Better yet, a picture of my pouting corpse laid out in Reg Ryan's would be sent to them. Draper Doyle, dead at last. Later to be buried in Orphan's Corner at St. Martin's Cemetery, my mother having posthumously disowned me.

"Hold out your hand," he said, and smiled the way he had so often smiled at me after strapping one of the other boys. He looked as if some greater wisdom was guiding both of us, as if he was doing no more than he had been instructed to do, and no more than I knew that I deserved. Here, finally, was the meaning of that smile. Our understanding had been not that I would never be strapped, but that it was inevitable that I would be, for it was in my very nature to deserve it.

"Your hand," he said. I shook my head, now realizing that this was what strapping was all about—the simple, wanton gesture of holding out your hand, seeming to do so willingly, offering your own hand for punishment as if there was no question of the rightness of what was being done, no question that you deserved it.

"Hold it out," he shouted, blinking rapidly. Again, I shook my head. He grabbed me by the arm and led me down the hall to his office, the door of which he closed behind us. "All right," he said, walking about the office as if in search of something, "all right." Then he stopped and faced me again.

"If you won't hold it out," he said, "I'll hold it out for you." He reached down and, as gently as if he wished to inspect it for injury, took my hand and slowly raised it, all the while looking at me. It was a strange pose, each of us standing with one arm held out to the other, my hand in his.

"Open your hand," he shouted. I shook my head. My hand was not closed in a fist. It was just that I had let it go limp, and it was lying half-open in his hand.

"Open it," he shouted. Shaking my head no, I began to cry.

"Crying," he said. "Crying and I haven't even started yet."

When I once again refused to open my hand, he told me he would strap me with it closed and it would probably hurt more. I said nothing. Slowly, deliberately, with his right hand, he raised his belt above his head, still holding my hand in his left, intending to hold it until the last moment, it seemed, in case I let it drop or pulled away. There we were, me standing with my back to the door, Father Seymour facing me, holding my hand, the belt raised high above his head, about to come down, when the door opened.

I knew, even before I turned around, that it was my mother, for no one else could have made him look so compromised; only being surprised by her in what must surely have been the least chivalrous of all possible circumstances could have made him look the way he did. I felt her put her hands on my shoulders and watched as, blinking rapidly, Father Seymour lowered his belt.

"Draper Doyle," my mother said, turning me around and guiding me towards the door.

"Mom—" I said.

"Go home," she said, and, before I had even had a chance to see her face, she was pushing me through the door. Knowing that she would wait until she heard me go down the stairs, I decided against putting my ear to the door.

Exactly what passed between them that afternoon, I never did find out. All I know is that later that day my mother came home to tell me that I was no longer a member of Father Seymour's Number. And you'd have thought that I had never been a member for how completely my mother's decision to withdraw me was ignored. Aunt Phil, when she came home, said nothing about it, nor ever afterwards made mention of it. My brief stint in Father Seymour's Number fell victim to the ongoing revision of the family history that had claimed, among other things, my father's missing year.

It's too bad that my even briefer stint as purchasing agent for St. Martin's Orphanage did not suffer the same fate. Aunt Phil got some measure of revenge by telling Sister Louise about the underwear when we were all sitting about the living room that night. A kind of impromptu party was held in my dishonour, a gathering at Aunt Phil's of all those people whose being apprised of the state of my underwear would most embarrass me.

No mention was made of any of the events of the day. Aunt Phil talked as if, having found out about my underwear purchases and my lying to the woman at Woolworth's, Father Seymour had simply relayed the information, leaving it to her and to my mother to take care of it. What especially bothered Aunt Phil and Sister Louise was not my wetting the bed, nor even my lying, but my buying underwear in secret, usurping the authority of grownups by buying my own drawers. And then there was what Sister Louise called "the extent of the deception."

"Why, it was going on for months," she said, almost in disbelief, as if she had thought it impossible for a child to do anything of which his elders were not aware. Sister Louise, regarding me with a kind of bewildered disappointment, allowed that my being fatherless might have something to do with it, but Aunt Phil was having none of that. Why, you had only to look at my advantages to know how preposterous, etc.,

etc. There seemed—perhaps it was just my imagination—to be an undercurrent of suspicion that my motive in the crime might have been other than the one which I confessed. For what other reason than to have clean underwear and to hide his dirties from his relatives would a boy spend one half of his yearly allowance on Stanfield's white, size small? As if in hope of finding the answer to this question, they all stared at me.

A discussion about the usurpation of authority by children of what Sister Louise called "the present generation" was just getting underway when Uncle Reginald intervened. How old did you have to be to buy underwear these days? Uncle Reginald asked me. Wasn't it illegal to sell underwear to minors? There was no telling what they might do with it. Why, he remembered how, when he was a boy, he and his friends would pool their money and then have some older boy buy them boxer shorts, which they took turns wearing. He wore a look of fond reminiscence as he wondered if there were still street bums outside of Woolworth's, begging change from customers in the hope of getting enough money to buy a pair of drawers.

I was forever grateful to Uncle Reginald for bailing me out, as well as to my mother who afterwards bought me twenty pairs of underwear the easy way—that is, all at one time—and simply left them on the bed where I would find them, never once making mention of them.

★

Despite my mother's rescue, despite the way Uncle Reginald disarmed my tormentors, I was still upset when I went to bed that night, still playing the day's events over and over in my mind. I could see Father Seymour's face as he prepared to strap me, his eyes blinking rapidly with spite as he ordered me to open up my hand.

It took me a long while to fall asleep, and when I did I dreamed that Momary, naked as always though this time trailing a black purse behind her, was pursuing me down Fleming Street at night, making remarks about my backside. "Look at his bum, Mary," said my mother's voice, "look at how it bounces when he runs." Far more spectacular, I suspected, was the way her breasts were bouncing as *she* ran. With one hand tightly clamping my Methuselah, I kept looking over my shoulder at her, staring at her bosom, so hilarious, so volatile, the nipples going up and down like large pink eyes in a head that was nodding rapidly, nodding "yes," it might have been, "yes, yes, yes, yes, yes."

"Draper Doyle," Momary said, "I want to kiss you, Draper Doyle." I looked back to see her right behind me, holding out towards my backside a long black feather, trying to tickle me with it so that I was forced to make a kind of bow of my body, to run with my shoulders thrust back, my groin thrust out in front of me as if I was trying desperately to keep a pair of pants from falling down, my feet fighting for balance, for, even as I ran forward, I was in danger of falling backwards.

"Help!" I screamed, "Help!" until I saw, just up ahead, *The Daily Chronicle*, where I knew my father was working. I ran inside, ran stark naked into the newsroom, which was empty. Even the machine room was quiet, the window dark. That left his office. I went to the door and, instead of knocking, opened it to find my father naked, in the arms of a Momary-like creature, female above the paraline but male below it, my mother from the waist up and, my Methuselah being unmistakable, me from the waist down, my bud as erect as Tom the doberman's had been.

The creature was holding my father from behind, his hands on his waist, bending him slightly forward, his little erect bud aimed unmistakably at his backside. "No!" I screamed, then woke up to find myself in mid-pee, my alarm cock going off and still as hard as that of the creature in the dream. I ran to the bathroom and, when I was finished, when I was coming back to bed, I remembered the incident the dream was based on, remembered another day from my missing week.

It had been just over a year ago that I had gone to the newsroom to surprise him in the middle of the night. I remembered lying in bed beforeheand, thinking of how the next day was his birthday. By ten p.m. the rest of the *Chronicle* staff was always either gone home or working upstairs in production, which meant that he would have to spend the first few hours of his birthday by himself, then come home to sleep away the next one third of it, after which, perhaps without having seen either me or Mary, he would have to go back to work. By ten o'clock, with two hours still left in his birthday, he would once again be by himself.

Thinking of the birthday card I had left for him on the kitchen table, I had an idea. I would put the card in the sermon envelope and take it to him at the newsroom. Wouldn't he be surprised to see me, out after midnight, apparently delivering a sermon.

I managed to stay awake until about twelve-thirty when I got up, put on my clothes, including my duffle coat and boots, and took the sermon envelope from beneath the mattress. I crept out of my room and, grabbing the birthday card from the table, left by the kitchen door.

I looked up at the sky. It was a clear, cold night, but because of the brightness of the moon, not many stars were visible. It occurred to me that I had never been out at this hour before. I had once tried to stay awake all night, to see if time really passed while I was sleeping, to confirm my suspicions that the so-called hours between bedtime and morning were just inventions of my father. I had sat up in bed, trying my hardest to stay awake. My father kept coming in to see how I was doing. "The watch that proved the night," he called it, even though I fell asleep long before morning. Of course, he said, I hadn't really proved that time passed while I was sleeping, only that it passed while I was awake. The other question was one that not even philosophers could prove. "You're fooling me," I said. He smiled. "Here's a riddle," he said. "I'll give you a whole day to solve it. Name something you've done a thousand times but cannot remember doing." The answer, of course, though I didn't get it, was fall asleep.

I walked until I reached the graveyard, then began to run. I ran past the darkened convent, the inside of which I had yet to see. Whenever I had gone to collect the sermon from Sister Louise, the nun who answered the door had always had me wait outside. As I ran, I tried and, for the umpteenth time, failed to imagine what Sister Louise looked like in her bed.

I ran past Reg Ryan's, where I knew two people were being waked, and where the clock out front read 12:43.

When I reached the *Chronicle*, the whole building was dark except for the lights on the second floor where production was in full swing. There were no windows in the newsroom, which was on the first floor, so I couldn't see my father. By now, all the copy would have been sent upstairs, and my father's job, until quitting time, would be to watch the wire in case of last-minute stories. This was the part of the day he hated most, for a story at this point might mean redoing the whole front page.

I went inside. At the end of the hall, the door of the newsroom was open and I could hear the occasional blast of static from the police-band radio which was said to have been playing non-stop since years before my father had joined the *Chronicle*. I ran down the hall and into the newsroom, with the sermon envelope held stop-the-presses style above my head, all set to shout "Happy Birthday" when I saw that the place was empty.

The window in the machine-room door was dark, so he was not in there either. Unless he was upstairs in production, the only other place was his office, which he almost never used and which, judging by the silence, was also empty.

I was about to go upstairs when I heard, from inside the office, what sounded like a chair scraping on the floor. Thinking my father had heard me and had just pushed back his chair to come out, I thought I would beat him to it. I ran to the door and, once again holding the envelope stop-the-presses style above my head, burst in, shouting "Happy Birthday," the punch line to a classic bit of slapstick, it turned out, for there, caught absurdly in the act, were my father and another man, engaged in what might have been some strange form of mimicry, their trousers down around their ankles, their shirt-tails and their ties hanging loose, my father bent over as if to read the teletype, with the other man bent over him, their pale and strangely naked bodies pressed urgently together, the other man with his arms wrapped round my father's chest, his head resting sideways on his back, and his eyes shut fervently against the world while my father, whose eyes were likewise closed, was holding, with his ink-stained hands, the back of a chair that was pushed against the wall, bracing himself against it, face bursting red from his exertions, grimacing with pain or pleasure, it was hard to tell.

They must have thought the door was locked, for it took them a moment to come blinking back to the world, to realize that they had been caught, let alone by whom. They turned to look at me, unable at first, because their eyes were still adjusting to the light, to make me out. I must have been, with the glare from the newsroom behind me, a mere shadow in the doorway. For what seemed like a very long time, my father squinted disbelievingly, as if, facing him in the doorway was a sight even less likely than that of his eight-year-old son, as if it was his other self that he was staring at and that was staring back at him, the Donald Ryan he had thought was home in bed but instead was hours early, strayed, like some sleepwalker from his other life, from the minds of his wife and children, to confront him. At first, as if to keep me from seeing how they were joined, they stayed exactly as they were; then, as if a scene which had begun as slapstick must end that way, they began to waddle towards me, my father's shirt-tail covering his front, the two of them moving so perfectly in time that my father might have been standing on the other man's feet. My father reached out with one hand as if to touch me, but instead took hold of the door and, without a word and barely giving me time to step backwards from the office, slammed it shut.

I dropped the envelope, then turned and ran. I ran from the newsroom, ran down the stairs, and out the door. Instead of going back by Fleming Street, I took the long way home, walking past darkened houses in which, it was a comfort to know, people who had never heard of me were sleeping.

All that had happened over a year ago. I turned off the light and got in bed. The Rhodes Blades. The Gay Blades. I wonder if that was the real joke in that photograph. It must have seemed to my father that the priesthood was his only hope. Instead, his father allowed him four years at Oxford, a stay of marriage, four years, perhaps, of the kind of life he could never keep secret at home, the kind of life from which he had hoped the priesthood would preserve him. Perhaps he had thought it was something he could rid himself of by indulging in it for a time, get it out of his system, and return home the young man they all wanted him to be. Or else it was four years of resisting that life, the toll of the struggle being such that, had he been at home, his family would have noticed that something was terribly wrong and his secret might have been discovered. You couldn't expect to wrestle with such a demon and at the same time keep him hidden from the world. Not for long, anyway.

And then the missing year. Had he planned to stay away forever and changed his mind? Had he been afraid to come straight
home, needing some time to ease back into being Donald
Ryan? I tried to imagine him in Montreal. For a year he had
watched them, the Divine Ryans, from his hiding place. For a
year, he had crept in memory about the old house on Fleming
Street, his house, peeking through the windows at his family.
And one night, his face pressed to the glass, watching his family
who as good as thought him dead, going on without him, he
could not resist returning, showing up one day at the door, the
prodigal come home, the son who was dead come back to life.

16

DESPITE THE great season they had had, despite Bobby Hull and his time-travelling slapshot, the Chicago Black Hawks were defeated by the Leafs in six games in the semi-finals, paving the way, it seemed, to another easy Cup for Montreal, who had beaten the Rangers in four games. The Leafs, whose victory over the mighty Black Hawks was seen as a fluke, were supposed to be easy pickings for the Habs. All we had to do to win the Cup, said Uncle Reginald, was beat the Leafs, the aging, decrepit, 1967 Maple Leafs, by common consent the worst team ever to make it to the Stanley Cup finals.

He devoted a full session of oralysis to the awfulness of the 1967 Maple Leafs. He told me that the Leafs' goalie, Johnny Bower, whose age was officially listed as forty-two, was rumoured to have a son who had retired from some minor professional league because of old age. That meant Bower could not be less than fifty-five and might conceivably be sixty-five or sixty-six. Uncle Reginald went around the room singing "Ole Man Bower" to the tune of "Ole Man River." On top of this, the Leafs had one other player over forty, five others over thirty-five, and five others over thirty. How could the Habs lose to such a team? The Leafs looked like some industrial-league team, he said, bald heads and pot bellies everywhere. They should have been wearing scarves and smoking pipes. How could such a team beat the fleet Canadiens, the likes of Beliveau, Duff, Rousseau, Cournoyer, Tremblay?

Who would have guessed that, after the fifth game of the Stanley Cup finals, the Leafs would be ahead three games to two? But then, even at that point, no one, not even Toronto fans, doubted that Montreal would come back. Even with our team down 3 – 2, and the next game to take place in Toronto, Uncle Reginald and I were still making jokes about the Leafs.

We compared Bobby Hull's slap-shot to Bobby Baun's.

"Bobby Baun's shot can barely travel through space," said Uncle Reginald, "let alone time."

"What's harder to find than Bobby Baun's hair?" I asked Uncle Reginald. He shrugged.

"Johnny Bower's birth certificate," I said.

"Johnny Bower is so old," said Uncle Reginald, "that there is a picture of him in the bible, herding sheep with his goalie stick. No wonder he's the only person in the world whose face is more wrinkled than his Methuselah."

Aunt Phil was just as optimistic about the Habs' chances as we were, despite the fact that Millie Barter was leading 3 – 2 on the knellephone. After the last game, a Leaf victory on Forum ice, Millie had broken the rules by letting Aunt Phil's phone ring seven times. But Aunt Phil was counting on the Habs to turn the tables and win one at Maple Leaf Gardens, after which, she said, she would let Millie's phone ring right off the wall. Then it would be back to the Forum for the Habs' third straight Stanley Cup—the last "real" Stanley Cup, Uncle Reginald called it, because the NHL was planning to expand from six to twelve teams before next season.

Aunt Phil announced, as if it guaranteed our victory, that Father Francis, who was just back from South America for a few months' rest, would be joining us to watch the sixth game. We should do our best to make him feel comfortable, she said. A social gathering was a rare thing for him, as was any sort of "luxury," as she put it. Television, radio, cars, electricity, these things were unheard of where Father Francis lived, so he might feel out of place for a while. The problem with Father Francis, she said, was that he was "too good for his own good." He worried so much about other people he forgot to worry about himself. What was missing from his character was a little selfishness, she said. That was what the evening would be then, an evening of rare selfishness for Father Francis.

Aunt Phil reminded everyone, but me most pointedly, that Father Francis might keep his hood up throughout the game. He would not feel awkward about it, she said, unless we did, so we should make every effort to seem relaxed. "Take no more notice of him than you would take of anyone else," Aunt Phil said.

This, as it turned out, was not so easy to do. The game had already started when Father Francis arrived, and those of us who had not seen him since he arrived home had to stop watching to shake his hand and exchange pleasantries with him. "Hello, my Newfie nephew," he said, as he shook my hand. "Hello, Father," I said, trying, as much for the Habs' sake as for his, not to become preoccupied with his hood, within which his face was barely visible. Though he was about the same height as Father Seymour, he was otherwise his opposite, his body faintly hunched, his arms, where they extended from his habit, thin and hairless.

By the time he was settled in, the first period was over and the Habs were losing 1 – 0. If a watched pot will never boil, an unwatched team will never win, I felt like saying, but something about his hood forbade such comments. It wasn't so bad when you could see his face, but when you couldn't and the hood had that empty, faceless, Grim Reaper look about it, it was hard to keep from staring.

What chance did we have of winning with Father Francis sitting there? Talk about the world's most unlikely hockey fan.

It was very off-putting, watching hockey with someone dressed the way he was. There we were, sitting around in Aunt Phil's living room, and there was this hooded figure, sitting among us. Anyone passing by on the street would have thought that Death had just dropped in to watch the game. By comparison, what Sister Louise and Father Seymour were wearing seemed quite normal—it might have been that in every living room on Fleming Street there were nuns and priests, and ours was remarkable only for having the hooded figure of Father Francis in it. There was no telling what would seem remarkable once we got used to Father Francis, I told myself, trying at the same time to concentrate on the game.

Aunt Phil and Sister Louise made a great show of not being at all bothered by the hood, and invited us by their expressions to do likewise, but I couldn't help myself. I soon came to think of Father Francis as a bad omen, not only because of how he looked, but because more attention was being paid to him than to the game. The occasion was not the sixth game of the Stanley Cup final, but the first visit by Father Francis since my father had died. There was no way a team could win when their fans were as preoccupied as we were.

Aunt Phil had obviously hoped that the presence of Father Francis would have an effect on my mother, that in the company of someone who thought she was still her old self she might go back to being her old self. It was soon apparent, however, that this would not happen. If anything, in fact, the tension between my mother and her inlaws was that much more pronounced with Father Francis there.

Father Francis himself said very little, replying with a few words when spoken to, accepting whatever was offered him in the way of refreshments, but otherwise just sitting there, his hands on the arms of his chair. Aunt Phil, as if she took his falling silent to mean that he was lapsing into unselfishness again, would jump up to fix him a cup of tea and something else to eat. The more obvious it became that something was wrong, the more Aunt Phil tried to act as if nothing was, and the more she made Father Francis the focus of attention. Nothing could happen, on TV or in the living room, but she must check his reaction to it. Was he pleased? Had he noticed that Montreal had scored to make it 2 − 1 for Toronto? Had he heard what Father Seymour said? Had he found it funny? Was he having a good time? It was clear, from his almost complete lack of response, that he either had no understanding of the game of hockey, or no interest in it, perhaps both. When Aunt Phil, of all people, took it upon herself to explain it to him, I knew there was no way the Habs would win.

In fact, by the start of the third period, I knew that all was lost. The mood in the house was far too dark, our attentions far too unfocussed, for even the Habs to make a comeback. There is a point in a game of hockey when you somehow know that no more scoring will take place. After the Leafs scored to make it 3 − 1, I knew this point had been reached. There would be no more scoring, I announced. I was as certain of it as if I was seeing replayed a game whose outcome I already knew. It was only a matter now of watching it, of staying with it until the end.

The only one who seemed not to understand that the game was over was Father Seymour. He began a kind of "I alone will not lose faith" routine, acting as if he was watching the game all by himself, cheering for a team that everyone else had given up for lost. Then, in the last few seconds, he went from being "the one true fan" to being "the one good sport," allowing to Mary and my mother, who were already celebrating, that the Leafs "deserved" to win.

When the game ended, Aunt Phil got up and turned off the television set, sparing us the sight of the Leafs skating about the

Gardens with the Cup. Then Uncle Reginald got up, took the phone from on top of the television set and, holding it on one hand as a waiter would hold a tray, delivered it to Aunt Phil, bowing slightly as, looking somewhat puzzled, she took it from him. That this was as good as saying that the Habs' defeat was her fault, Aunt Phil soon realized. Despite protests from Mary and my mother, she quite calmly pulled the phone plug from the wall. Then, just as calmly, almost matter-of-factly, she left the living room, taking the phone with her so that no one could reconnect it. It's a sight I will never forget, Aunt Phil marching down the hall with the telephone tucked beneath one arm, the cord trailing on the floor behind her. When we heard her room door closing, we all stood up.

Uncle Reginald left first, going down the hall, then stepping sombrely into the lift, ascending without a word to anyone. When my mother offered to help take Sister Louise back to the convent, Father Seymour assured her that he and Father Francis could manage. As he was putting on his coat, Father Seymour tousled my hair, smiling as if at some classic bit of boyishness when I pulled away. I tried to see if the Habs' defeat had in any way registered on Father Francis, but I couldn't quite see his face inside the hood. "See you next week," he said.

The notion that, although the Habs had just lost the Cup, the world was going on as usual was more than I could bear. People walking one another home, people putting on coats, people talking about next week—surely, it seemed to me, there would be no next week.

I went down the hall to my room and, for a while, sat there in the darkness, wondering how the Habs had lost. Then I looked out the window, thinking that this was a likely time for my father to appear, but the house across the way was dark, the backyard empty. I went to my bureau and, opening the bottom drawer, took out *The Cartoon Virgil.* Using the pen my father had used, the one without any ink, I wrote the score of the game on the cover. Toronto 3 – Montreal 1. 02/05/67. Then I got into bed.

When I closed my eyes, it was not the hockey game I saw, but something else. I saw my father as I had last seen him alive. I saw the other man's face pressed against his back, his cheek to my father's back, the two men with their eyes closed as if they were inwardly pursuing some common goal, something that was always just ahead of them, just out of reach. My father's face had been contorted as much with anguish as with pleasure, and no wonder. Faced with a choice that would have satisfied even Aunt Phil's grim sense of irony—misery in this life, or eternal damnation in the next—he had chosen damnation, through which, even as I was watching, he might have been bearing the other man on his back.

✦

I pulled the blankets up to my chin. "Something you have done a thousand times but cannot remember." Falling asleep. "You can't even dream of falling asleep," my father said. "But no dream seems more real than the dream of waking up." Waking. Why, I wondered, were the days that the dead lay on display in their caskets known as "wakes?" Waking up. How strange, to return to the world with no memory of having left it. Stranger still to dream of doing it.

I dreamed that I woke to the sound of a loud drumming on the roof. When I got up and looked out the window, hockey pucks were falling everywhere, falling straight down so that, although the windows of the houses were still intact, those of the cars parked along Fleming Street had been smashed in, as had most of the streetlamps, leaving the neighbourhood in almost total darkness. Fleming Street was black with pucks, teeming with them when Reg Ryan's funeral coach, drawn by four horses and driven by Uncle Reginald, pulled up behind the house. Uncle Reginald, dressed in his top-hat and tails, was shielding himself with a black umbrella, no ordinary umbrella, it seemed, by the way the pucks were bouncing from it. Though the horses were being pelted, they seemed not to mind or even notice. I opened the window, put my head as far out as I dared and shouted to him. "What's happening?" I said.

Above the roar of the falling pucks, as though from a great distance, I heard him say, "It's the Apuckalypse. The Apuckalypse has come. Just like your father said it would."

He pointed up.

"See," he said, "the sky is already turning blue."

"What should we do?" I shouted.

"You have to come with me," he said. "Put on your goalie equipment and come with me."

I got my equipment out of the closet and put it on, helmet, mask, chest protector, pads, even skates, then lumbered to the window. Uncle Reginald motioned with his arm for me to join him. It took me a long time to squeeze through the window, but I managed it. At the last second I lost my balance and more or less tumbled from the window sill, my fall broken by the pucks which lay about a foot deep on the ground. As soon as I emerged from beneath the eaves of the house, I was pelted with pucks. I made a shield with my blocker and my goalie stick and ran, the pucks slithering beneath my skates, the pads weighing me down so that I fell frequently, getting up in a panic for fear of being buried by the pucks, the worst possible fate for a goalie, it seemed to me. The thought of suffocating in the folds of the great black shroud of pucks that lay on the ground made me run that much faster.

When I got to the coach, Uncle Reginald reached down

one hand to help me up, then let me share his umbrella. I huddled against him, sobbing with panic, yet at the same time wondering if any goalie had ever faced this many shots before. Uncle Reginald turned the coach around, the horses highstepping through the pucks, then headed down Fleming Street.

"Where are we going?" I said.

"You have to stop the pucks," he said.

"Me?" I said.

"You," he said. "Only a goalie can do it."

"How do I stop them?" I said. He said nothing. He drove in silence until we reached Reg Ryan's, where he turned into the parking lot, stopping at the back of the home by the visitors' entrance. Out front, Reg Ryan's clock was dark, still showing the time at which it had been smashed out by the pucks—2:15.

Uncle Reginald dropped the reins. "In we go," he said.

"In there?" I said. "How will I stop the pucks in there?"

"Come on," he said, "we have to hurry." We jumped down from the coach, huddling beneath the umbrella as we waded through the pucks to the door.

"Oh," said Uncle Reginald, "I almost forgot. You'll need three pucks that haven't touched the ground." Stretching forth my glove, I caught one of the pucks as it was falling.

"Good glove hand," said Uncle Reginald.

I caught two more, then stuffed all three down in my goalie pads. Uncle Reginald opened the door and we stepped into the vestibule.

"What now?" I said.

"Now," said Uncle Reginald, closing his umbrella, a strange smile on his face, "you have to go downstairs. But first you have to sign the book."

Dropping my stick and my blocker, I made for the Visitors' Book, but Uncle Reginald shook his head. "Not that one," he said. I looked at him.

"This one," he said, and he pointed to the other side of the vestibule, where the Doomsday Book lay open on a lectern.

"Do I have to?" I said.

"You'll be the first person ever to sign his own name in the Doomsday Book," he said. I shook my head.

"Sign," he said, holding out to me a huge feathered quill. I took it from him and signed my name beneath that of the last person to be waked at Reg Ryan's, a person who, for all I knew, was downstairs at this very moment.

"Don't worry," said Uncle Reginald, "if you make it back, I'll rub it out." Before I had time to ask him what he meant by "if," a great roar sounded from the darkness at the bottom of the stairs, and a dog that looked strangely familiar came bounding up to meet me. It was Tom the doberman, or rather, a kind of *Classics Illustrated* version of him, five times his normal size and looking even larger, when at the top step he stood on his hind legs and flailed his forelegs in front of him. Instead of three heads, he had three sets of private parts. He was like some gross caricature of desire, the style as vulgar, as archly overstated, as that of cartoon propaganda—a cartoon rendering of lust rearing up in front of me, Tom the doberman with all three sets of private parts wagging lewdly each time he moved and his black ears absurdly taped above his head.

I screamed and turned to run out the door, but Uncle Reginald grabbed hold of me. "You'll never make it home through all those pucks," he said. "And even if you did, the time remaining would be short. You have to go downstairs."

I turned around and looked at Tom.

"How can I get past him?" I said.

"Tom has an appetite for pucks," said Uncle Reginald. "Just throw him one." I reached into my goalie pads and took out a puck, at the sight of which Tom roared again, his great eyes rolling in his head as he lurched about on his hind legs. I threw it on the floor in front of him, at which he came down on four legs and with one bite gobbled it up, except for some crumbs of rubber which fell from his mouth and which he afterwards licked up with his tongue, sniffing at the floor in case he had missed any. Then he turned and went bounding down the stairs, disappearing once again into the darkness.

"Down you go," said Uncle Reginald, putting his hand on my back and easing me gently toward the stairs.

"What do I have to do?" I said.

"Just go down," he said, taking my goalie glove from me, "you won't need this."

I began my descent, wobbling uneasily on my skates. About halfway down, I missed a step and, in the effort to keep myself from falling, went running down the stairs into the darkness, my arms held out as though in tribute to it. I hit the floor with a crash but somehow kept my balance, my skates clumping on the hardwood floor. I stopped, and as my eyes began adjusting to the darkness I saw that I was no longer at Reg Ryan's, but in our old house, which looked exactly as it had before we had moved out, before the carpenters had started work. For some reason, I found this more terrifying than if I had stumbled headlong into the red room.

"Uncle Reginald," I screamed, "Uncle Reginald, let me come back up." I could barely make him out at the top of the stairs. He shook his head, pointing to the window behind him, which was turning faintly blue. Suddenly the sound of the pucks falling on the roof grew louder; it might have been a drum roll, as if something momentous was about to happen.

"There's not much time," said Uncle Reginald.

"What am I supposed to do?" I shouted.

"Go down the hall," he said.

The end of the hall was so dark, I wondered if Tom the doberman might be waiting there. My skates once again clumping on the hardwood floor, I went down the hall until Uncle Reginald said "Stop." I stood between two doors, one blue, one red. Above the red door was a sign which said "The Fields of Mourning."

"I don't want to go in there," I said.

No sooner were the words out of my mouth than the blue door swung open and the boys of Father Seymour's Number came marching out, some shadowboxing, some tap-dancing, all singing, doing a kind of garbled, dream rendition of "Ave Maria." They went jabbing, feinting, dancing past me, then in a circle around me, all wearing the same eager-to-please expressions, all wearing a kind of hybrid uniform, dressed like dancers above the waist and like boxers below.

"What's going on?" I said.

"Your descendants," said Uncle Reginald, who was suddenly standing right beside me. "Unless you go in there." He pointed to the red door.

"All right," I said. As if on cue, the circle broke, and the boys of Father Seymour's Number went back from where they came, the blue door slamming shut behind them.

I turned, and, wondering why the sign said "The Fields of Mourning," opened the red door and stepped inside.

"Uncle Reginald!" I screamed. Although it was dark, I could see against the wall a sofa on which my father was laid out, his hands clasping what looked like a prayer book to his chest. The pose was the same as in the Morenz dream, as if they were waking him on the sofa instead of in a casket. He was even dressed the same, in a tuxedo with a ruffled front, and had his hair slicked back. Was this what I had come for, I wondered, to look for the second time at my dead father, to give him, perhaps, the kiss I was supposed to have given him before?

"I don't want to kiss him!" I shouted, looking over my shoulder.

"You don't have to," said Uncle Reginald, who was standing in the doorway as if to block any escape I might try to make. "Just go to the sofa and turn on the light."

I was hardly more inclined to do this, but I walked across the room. Suspended from the ceiling above the sofa was a lamp like the one in the red room, placed to shed a kind of celestial light on the face of the person in the casket. I reached up, pulled the silver chain that was hanging from it, then jumped back in horror, for my father's eyes, as if the two things were controlled by the same mechanism, had come open when the light came on. I turned around, covered my own eyes, and began to scream.

"Please, let me go back up. Please," I said.

"Crying is not going to work," said Uncle Reginald. "Now turn off that light."

I faced the sofa once again and, taking care to avoid looking at my father's eyes, reached up and pulled the chain. The light went off and when I worked up the nerve to look, I saw that my father's eyes were closed. I made as if to leave, but Uncle Reginald held up his hands. "Not yet," he said, "you have to keep his eyes from coming open."

"But as long as the light is off—"

"It comes on by itself," he said.

"I don't want to touch him," I said. "I'm not touching him."

"You don't have to," said Uncle Reginald. "Just use the pucks."

"What?" I said.

"The pucks," he said. "Put them on his eyes."

I reached into my pads and took out the two remaining pucks.

"Put them on his eyes?" I said.

Nodding his head and looking at me through circles made from his thumbs and index fingers, Uncle Reginald said gravely, "*On his eyes.*"

Making sure that no part of me came into contact with my father, I laid them gingerly, first one puck, then the other, on his eyes. He looked almost comical, as if he was wearing shades to help him sleep.

"There," said Uncle Reginald. "Even if his eyes come open, he'll never see through those."

Once again I turned to leave and once again Uncle Reginald held up his hands. "Not yet," he said, "you need the book."

I looked at the black book my father was clasping to his chest.

"What for?" I said.

"*The book*," said Uncle Reginald.

Enough of the book was exposed that I could take hold of it without touching my father's hands. I pulled, gently at first, for fear of dislodging the pucks, but I couldn't tear it loose.

"Pull harder," said Uncle Reginald. "He doesn't want to let it go."

I pulled as hard as I dared, all the while staring at the pucks, which stayed in place. Finally, the book came free and I went stumbling backwards, straight into the arms of Uncle Reginald.

"I'll hold that for you," he said, taking the book from me. "You'll need both your hands to get back up."

We left my father lying there, with two hockey pucks weighting down his eyes.

As I was about to follow Uncle Reginald up the stairs, the blue door opened and Young Leonard came out, holding what appeared to be a glass of water. "Before you go back up," Young Leonard said, "you must drink this."

"What is it?" I said.

"A draught of long oblivion," Young Leonard said. I took it from him and was just about to drink it when Uncle Reginald came running down the stairs and knocked it from my hand.

"Come on," he said. This time, as we ascended, he kept looking behind him to make sure that I was following. When he reached the top step, he turned around and screamed "Watch out."

Suddenly, standing in front of me, blocking my way to the landing, was Tom the doberman, his roar ten times as loud as before. Lurching on his hind legs, his three sets of private parts bobbing in front of him, he began coming down the stairs. I reached into my goalie pads for another puck, only to find that there was none.

"Uncle Reginald," I screamed, unable to see him, for Tom the doberman had stopped on the step just above mine, his flailing forepaws scissoring about my head.

"You said I would need three pucks," I shouted. "You should have said four. Now I can't get back up."

"Ask you-know-who what to do," said Uncle Reginald, peeking out at me from behind Tom.

"Who, him?" I said incredulously, pointing at the dog.

Uncle Reginald rolled his eyes. "No," he said, "Methuselah. Ask your Methuselah what to do."

"No way," I said. "Not here, not on the stairs. They'll see me."

"Who'll see you?" said Uncle Reginald.

"Mom and Mary," I said, pointing to the doors on the landing.

"Now is no time for bashfulness," said Uncle Reginald. Tom roared again.

"OK," I said, "OK, I'll do it." Looking nervously past Tom to make sure that the doors on the landing were still closed, I took off my sweater, my chest protector, my skates, my goalie pads, my hockey pants, my underwear and jock. There I was, naked except for my mask.

"I need a mirror," I screamed, "I need a mirror."

Just then, the doors opened and out came Mary and my mother.

"Look," Mary screamed, her hand over her mouth. "Look at Draper Doyle's Methuselah. It must be a million years old."

How like Mary it was, with Tom standing there five times his normal size, his ears taped up above his head, his three pairs of private parts bouncing up and down, to notice my Methuselah instead.

"Shutup, Mary," I said. "Mary, Mary, bum so hairy, how do you make it grow?"

"Ya know what it looks like, Draper Doyle?" said Mary. "It looks like a pair of prunes."

I glanced at my mother, who was standing there, trying to hide a smile, staring with a kind of affectionate glee at my Methuselah—my puny Methuselah, her expression seemed to say.

"Mom, I need a mirror," I said.

"Are you sure you want to see yourself?" she said, at which she and Mary went into fits of laughter.

"Yes," I said, "I'm sure. A small mirror. Get me your compact." She did as I said, reaching around Tom the doberman to throw the compact to me.

"I don't know, Draper Doyle," Mary said. "I don't think any amount of makeup is going to make that look any better."

I turned my back to them and, bending over, held the mirror between my legs, moving it about until, at last, I saw the Great Hairless One staring back at me. "Oh Methuselah," I said, "oh Great Hairless One, oh Great Wrinkled One, oh Oracle of Oracles, oh Prune of Prunes, oh Wisest of the Wise, tell me all."

"What is your question?" said Methuselah.

"How do I get past Tom?" I said. "I'm out of pucks."

"You must kiss her," said Methuselah.

"Kiss who?" I said.

"Her," said Methuselah.

I was about to ask him if he meant Mary or my mother, when Uncle Reginald, pointing to where they had been standing, shouted "Her!" There she was, standing as tall as Tom the doberman, stark naked on the landing—Momary, top-heavy with my mother's breasts and swaying uncertainly on Mary's little legs, Momary with two belly buttons, one above the paraline and one below.

Tom the doberman, ears and private parts erect, turned around, then stepped up on the landing to face Momary. Prancing about on his two hind legs, flailing his forepaws as if inviting Momary to box, he put back his head and gave a roar that shook the house.

Momary, however, ignored him, waddled around him, and came, breasts bouncing, down the stairs. Stopping in front of me, looming over me like some great spectacle of nakedness, she spoke. "Got a kiss for me, Draper Doyle?" she said. It was Mary's voice, coming from my mother's mouth.

I knew I didn't have much choice. It was either kiss her, assuming that a kiss was all she wanted, or let Tom have his way with me. Or else stay down here forever. "Hell, hellhound, or Momary," was how Uncle Reginald summed up my choices.

"Momary," I said.

"In that case," said Uncle Reginald, smiling, "I'll erase your name from the Doomsday Book."

I watched as, using his forefinger, he erased my name. Even so, a kind of ghost of it remained, my signature indented in the page. "We'll shade it in when you come back," he said.

There we stood, Momary and me. My little boy's private parts, my bud and my Methuselah, were showing, and I was staring straight at the beard between her legs, while her breasts formed a kind of canopy above my head. Lips puckered, eyes closed, Momary began bending from the waist. Her breasts came down and for the briefest of moments my head was wedged between them; their warm, sweet softness brushed against my ears, my cheeks. And then her face was looming over me, in front of me, my mother's face, eyes closed, lips puckered in a kind of parody of rapture. "Kiss me, Draper Doyle," said Mary's voice, as Momary reached out and, before I could protest, took off my mask.

I puckered my own lips, closed my eyes and eased my face forward, further forward, until I found her, felt her in the darkness, kissing me, but at the same time somehow resisting, pulling away just enough to make me follow her, falling slowly backwards so that to keep my lips on hers, I too was forced to fall; soon, I was lying prone, on top of her it seemed, though I still felt nothing; there might have been nothing left of her but her lips, and nothing left of me but mine, hers holding mine up in the darkness, keeping them afloat. And then hers vanished, disappeared from under mine and, as a kind of body awareness returned to me, I began to fall, suddenly, precipitously, plunging downwards. I curled up to shield myself, drew my knees up to my head and wrapped my arms around them, bracing for some impact, some collision.

I was balled up in this manner when I awoke, this time for real. My first thought was that I was once again in mid-pee. I raised the sheet, pulled my underwear out from my stomach. There was my bud, looking as though it had just keeled over from exhaustion, a little white tongue hanging from its mouth. After nine years of producing nothing but pee, it had, by some leap, by some strange innovation, managed this. Whatever "this" might be, for I had no idea. (Just how much of a leap it was, I would not fully understand until the next time it happened, which was not until three years later.) The moment I touched it, the moment I began rubbing that strange stuff between my fingers, I remembered.

The whole thing had taken but a minute. I had woken up, gone downstairs, as in the dream, to find my father, and find him I did, in the living room, staring in what might have been wide-eyed amazement at the ceiling. Not even for a moment had I mistaken him to be alive. The book which, in the dream, had been a prayer book, was *The Cartoon Virgil*, and I remembered having had to pry it from his hands, so tightly was he holding it. Then I had gone back upstairs and, strange though it may seem, back to sleep.

A brief, dream-like interval was all it was, an interval with sleep on either side, two pools of sleep that at my bidding had overflown, wiping out that strand of time, that mere moment that lay between.

Later, I woke to hear someone locking my bedroom door from the outside. I had no idea why the door was being locked. I can still remember the sound of the key turning slowly, then the sound of footsteps across the landing as whoever it was went to Mary's door.

I don't know who crept up the stairs to lock our doors. It might have been my mother, but it might also have been Aunt Phil who, having let herself in, found my father before my mother was even out of bed. "I found him first," Aunt Phil kept saying afterwards, as if, by doing so, she had reclaimed him for the Ryans.

Not long after I heard the key, I heard Mary banging on her door, shouting to me, and then to my mother, to let her out. When no one came, she shouted louder, and finally began to scream, beating her fists on the door, then on the wall that joined our rooms, even on the floor, because her door was locked, because, at six in the morning, there were strangers in the house, strangers whose voices she could hear, but whose words she could not make out.

I heard, until I could stand it no longer, the somehow

shameful sound of footsteps from below, the sound of hushed whispering and someone crying. Then I climbed beneath the blankets and, putting my hands about my ears, closed my eyes and, without even knowing it, tried very, very hard to keep another pair of eyes from coming open.

It had taken over a year for my memory of those events to be restored. I got out of bed and went to the window. I was relieved to see that pucks were neither falling nor piled three feet deep on the ground. The first light of day was in the sky, though the streetlamps were still burning and no traffic was moving on Fleming Street. "We'll shade it in when you come back," Uncle Reginald had said. I looked at *The Cartoon Virgil* on the dresser. For a moment, I thought I had only dreamed of writing the score of last night's game on the cover. Why had my father had it in his hands when I found him? I wondered. There had been no sign of any piece of paper that he might have been shading to find the scores, something that a man in such circumstances might well have done as a way of remembering the past, of looking back, one last time, on the life that he had lived.

Taking a piece of paper from one of my school scribblers, I put it on the book, then began to shade it slowly from the top with a pencil. The scores of games played years ago began appearing, emerging ghostly from the paper. Also, however, like some buried memory at long last surfacing, these words appeared: "Dear Draper Doyle." I stopped shading and it occurred to me that, if I destroyed the book now, I would never have to know what came next. Yet even as I thought about how I might destroy the book, I continued shading, going slowly down the page, from left to right, revealing the words in the order he had written them, as if, at that very moment, he was writing them.

How long have I been dead? Have I been buried yet? Did they tell you how I died? If they didn't, you know now. If by this time, you haven't told them what you saw, don't bother. No one but your mother would believe you, and unless I miss my guess, she already has her suspicions. I won't try to explain it to you, Draper Doyle. I won't even ask you to forgive me. I have come to believe that there is no such thing as forgiveness. You will all be better off without me. Believe me. Whatever chance you three had for happiness is that much greater now that I am gone.

It was a few bewildering moments before I realized that this letter had been written, not after, but before my father's death, not by my father's ghost, but by my father. He had written his suicide note to me on the cover of *The Cartoon Virgil*, and had left my finding it, my ever finding it, to chance.

I jumped out of bed and ran to the window, thinking my father might be watching from the kitchen across the way. There were no lights on in the house, however, nor was my father in the yard. I leaned my forehead against the glass and began to cry, more for us, for my mother, Mary, and me, than for my father whom I had hardly known.

For how long before he died had my father been free from the marriage bed? I wondered. Perhaps since I was born. His relief at hearing that I was a boy must have been even greater than Aunt Phil's or Father Seymour's. His duty done. And for how long before he died had he been in that other bed? Possibly since before his marriage, but more likely since his breakdown. Between my finding them at the newsroom and my finding him downstairs, there had been only a few hours, hardly time enough for him to think about doing what he did. But then, this was not surprising, given that ever facing me again must have seemed out of the question. He may even have made his mind up years before, carried around with him like some cyanide capsule the knowledge of what he must do if he was caught.

Leaving *The Cartoon Virgil* on the bed, I went down the hall to my mother's room. Her door was slightly open, so I was able to watch her sleeping, her long, young woman's legs moving slowly beneath the blankets. Her head was turned as if she was looking out the window, as if, unable to sleep, she was staring at the streetlamp, but her eyes were closed. "She already has her suspicions." Had she guessed his secret and blamed herself for it? Had it been from guilt, even more than from grief, that she had lately emerged, escaped, to go running for her life down Fleming Street? "Do you, Donald Ryan, take that tall Delaney girl to be your wife?" It seemed strange to think that, if my father had not been forced to a life that would lead him to suicide, Mary and I would never have been born.

Looking at my mother, it occurred to me that there was one way out, something which, even if she thought of it, she would never do. But then, I could do it just as well. I could go now to Aunt Phil's room and say what I knew my mother would never say.

Going down the hall, it crossed my mind that to barge into the bedroom of someone who believed in visitations the way that Aunt Phil did was a cruel thing to do. On the other hand, this was the only way I could be alone with her. Aunt Phil was not the kind of woman that a nine-year-old could ask to have a word with privately. I knelt down outside her door and, closing one eye, put the other to the keyhole, at the same time placing both hands against the door which, even before my eye had begun to focus on the scene in front of it, gave way, opening inward with the most mournful of sounds, leaving me to fall prostrate on the floor.

Aunt Phil must have thought someone had kicked the door down, so loudly did it crash against the wall. I was sure that

Mary and my mother would come running, but they didn't. Nor was Aunt Phil quick in reacting. I heard a great inhalation of breath, which she held for what seemed an impossible length of time, as if she dared not let it out. Was she sitting up in bed, I wondered, unable to see me, perhaps waiting for whoever had opened the door in such dramatic fashion to make an equally dramatic entrance? Was she, even as I lay there on the floor, expecting Him? That would explain the way she looked when I got up—half terrified, half puzzled, she might have been wondering why, instead of looming over her, the ghost of her dead husband was less than five feet tall.

Poor Aunt Phil. She was not accustomed to being awakened by anything but her own body's built-in, infallible alarm clock, which was set for all eternity at five a.m. What, in that first moment, she had taken me to be, is hard to say, but she soon recovered. "Draper Doyle," she said. No more unlikely projection of her conscience could be imagined, I suppose, than that of her nine-year-old nephew, Draper Doyle, but there I was at the foot of her bed in the middle of the night, come to accuse her. She seemed to relax a bit: then, as if she had lapsed back into doubting my existence, she sat up, retreated a little against the pillows, and squinted at me.

"Draper Doyle," she said again, this time more boldly, as if she hoped her next word would send me running from the room. Before she could speak again, I closed the door.

"What on earth?" she said, and was halfway out of bed before I spoke.

"I know about Dad," I said. She stopped, and though with the door closed I could no longer see her face, I could tell by the sudden sagging of her body that she understood me. Now that there was no turning back, I felt less afraid. I looked at her lying there, half out of bed, in a nightdress which hung down below her knees, and a hairnet which, I realized, was the secret of why her hair always had that pressed down, moulded look about it.

For what seemed like a very long time, she stayed there on the edge of the bed, staring at me so hard that I was grateful for the darkness. Then she raised one hand to her mouth. "I've thought of the devil as being many things," she whispered.

"I know about Dad," I said. "He wrote me a letter. I never found it until today."

"You don't even understand what you're saying, Draper Doyle," she said, in a coaxing and somewhat relieved tone of voice, as if this "letter" might be no more than the latest figment of my imagination.

"I know what he did," I said. "But I won't tell anyone, not if you let us go away. I won't even say anything to Mary."

I still couldn't see her face, but I could tell by the way she straightened up that she was gathering herself for something. Then a kind of shrill sigh escaped from her and her shoulders sagged again.

"Promise?" I said. I had expected it would take much more, had thought it possible, even likely, that she would make such a fuss that the others would hear her and come running. I hadn't realized—how could I, at the age of nine, have realized?—the kind of advantage I had over her, the kind of position I had her in. Far from refusing me, she dared not even force me to tell *her* what I knew, dared not bring the family secret even so close to the light of day as to make me say it. Though she was faced with having to trust a nine-year-old who might not have the sense to keep his word, she could take no chances, a fact she acknowledged, not by saying anything, but merely by getting back into bed, and pulling the covers up over her.

"Promise?" I said.

"Go back to bed," she said, settling down beneath the blankets. "And close the door behind you."

I wondered if, in the morning, she might think the whole thing had been a dream.

GUESS WHO was nice enough to lend us the money to move away?" my mother said, wiping tears from her eyes.

"Not Aunt Phil?" Mary said.

"Yes," my mother said, shrugging with mystification but smiling at the same time, "Aunt Phil."

"Aunt Phil?" Mary said again, looking at me with astonishment, an expression I was soon mimicking, shaking my head as if I was every bit as amazed as she was, but all the while wondering what Aunt Phil had had to mortgage to get rid of me.

★

The only thing Aunt Phil asked from my mother was that she grant my father a kind of posthumous divorce by resuming her maiden name. Henceforth, my mother told us, our last name would be Delaney. It seemed that our divinity had lapsed. I suspected that not long after we were gone, it would be as though Donald Ryan had never married. Or that, at least, would have been the case if not for Uncle Reginald who, when I invited him to come with us, declined. "I'm not letting them off that easy," he said.

We had to wait until the end of the school year before we left. Given what our stay with Aunt Phil had been like, that last month didn't seem so bad. Aunt Phil and I tacitly agreed to avoid each other, to acknowledge one another's existence only when we had to.

I decided not to take *The Cartoon Virgil* with me. One night, as the carpenters who were still working on our old house were getting ready to leave, I went over and, when no one was looking, pushed the book through one of the holes they had knocked in the plaster. It landed with a thud, and the next day the hole was blocked up with plaster once again. It may have been found by this time, or it may still be there, rotting like some skeleton between the walls.

But the puck, the one memento from my father's missing year, I still have. Looking out my bedroom window a few days before we left, I happened to see it embedded in a patch of mud. The pieces of paper which had been attached to it were gone, but the words my father had written were still there, faintly engraved in the puck so that I could shade them in when I wanted.

What Aunt Phil told Father Seymour, Father Francis, and Sister Louise to reconcile them to the fact that we were leaving, we never did find out. But in no time, the official family position was that it was a good idea. In fact, by the way they acted, it might have been their idea, one that, hard though it might be for us to accept, was in everyone's best interest.

The day that we left, they all came to Aunt Phil's to see us off, all hugged and kissed us as if the events of the past year had never happened. "Goodbye my dear," Father Seymour said as he kissed my mother on the cheek.

The plan had been for us to take a taxi to the airport, but Uncle Reginald wouldn't hear of it. He would, he said, take us to the airport in style, which is to say in his hearse. Aunt Phil protested against using the hearse in this manner—what if someone saw him driving it while out of uniform, she said. There was no chance of that, said Uncle Reginald, because he planned to wear his uniform. He had us wait while he took the lift upstairs. Ten minutes later, he came back down in coat and tails, his top-hat in his hands. "Ladies and gentleman," he said, "your hearse is waiting."

I had always figured that we would leave Fleming Street in a hearse, though I hadn't expected us all to go together, not to mention while we were still alive. Rather than climb into the casket compartment, which Aunt Phil wanted us to do so that no one on Fleming Street would see us, we all piled into the front seat with Uncle Reginald. More than one person on the route to the airport witnessed the unlikely sight of a woman and her two children, crammed like hitchhikers into the front seat of Reg Ryan's hearse, all laughing except for Uncle Reginald, whose mournful expression was even more pronounced than usual.

Why was it easier, Uncle Reginald wondered, to say good-bye to the dead than to the living? "You'll see us again," my mother said. Uncle Reginald shook his head. "So far," he said, "my record of not seeing my passengers again is perfect. I wouldn't want to spoil it." I told him I wished my record of not seeing his passengers again was perfect and he laughed. My father had not appeared to me, even in dreams, since the night the Leafs had won the Cup, so I knew the pucks were still in place and my father was still downstairs where he belonged.

At the airport, we got some strange stares when Uncle Reginald, looking grimly official in his waistcoat and top-hat, got out of the hearse, threw open the rear doors, and, pausing for effect, began to solemnly unload our luggage. There followed what may still be the only instance of people smothering the driver of a hearse with hugs and kisses.

Finally he stepped back, removed his hat, and giving us his best, most mournfully respectful bow, turned around, got in the hearse and drove away.

As the plane took off, as the city fell away and Mary and my mother crowded the window, searching the ground below for Fleming Street, I closed my eyes and replayed a scene from the day before. Walking down Fleming Street just after dark, I had spotted Mary and Harold Noonan, pressed against each other, Harold Noonan with his arms around Mary from behind so that it looked as if he had finally, literally, caught up with her, as if, while they were walking along with the usual fifty yards of street between them, he had increased his speed just enough to surprise her from behind, to catch her. They were hardly recognizable without that fifty yards between them.

It didn't seem, in any way, to be a passionate embrace. Mary's arms were at her sides and she was quite expressionless. The only sign that she was even aware of Harold's arms around her was that her eyes were closed. She might have been hoping that when she opened them, Harold would be gone. Harold on the other hand, though he was standing about as awkwardly as Mary, had his eyes open. He was staring wide-eyed down the street, as if he had bumped into Mary by accident and was wondering how, without acknowledging her existence, he could ask her to step aside. Still, he was holding her and she was letting him, there was no denying that. That long-haired, long-limbed Lothario from down the street, who appeared to be wearing a bunch of grapes on one side of his head, so long and lopsided was his hair, had my sister in his arms.

When their image disappeared, another one replaced it. I saw Tom the doberman, his ears absurdly taped above his head, sitting in the middle of Fleming Street. As I ran towards him, he began to run away, loping down the middle of the street, looking back at me now and then, keeping constant that distance between us. Tom, you dopey dog, I said. I may even have said it out loud. Tom, you cartoon hellhound, wait for me.

Wayne Johnston is the author of five novels, including most recently *The Colony of Unrequited Dreams*. He lives in Toronto.